Maple and Honey

Gerald D. Johnson

MAPLE AND HONEY

First edition. April 9, 2024.

ISBN: 979-8224746217

Written by Gerald Johnson.

Books also Written:

The Eye to My Storms

Alabama Sunrise

A Dream Deferred: Part One

Maple and Honey

ONE

On Saturday morning, Honey danced and sang, smelling the sweet aroma of the baked bread. Honey opened the oven to see the crispy brown dessert. The apple pie was almost ready.

The music of Motown blasted as she cleaned her stove top, humming to the beat of The Temptations, and when she heard Gladys Knight & the Pips, she increased the volume on the radio.

It reminded her of the good old days.

"Love Overboard!" she shouted, popping her shoulders and snapping her fingers.

Honey lived alone and was content until her best friend and neighbor, Maple, stopped by to chat or call her on the phone.

Maple's house sat on the corner across from hers, adjacent to a dead-end street.

Maple and Honey were single women in their sixties who lived jazzy lives. Their history would shock people and have them wondering if it was true. They carried themselves as modest queens, but 'back in the day,' as they called it, it was another story. Their story would pull people to the edge of their seats with their jaws dropped. However, they only shared a glimpse of their truth.

Maple would say, "People don't need to know your whole damn business."

A woman once told Honey, "There's no way you and Maple were prostitutes."

"Chile, yes we were," Honey said. "I was a bad woman, and I am not ashamed of my past," Honey said, and she meant it. She dared anybody to judge her about how she used to be. As far as Honey was concerned, her testimony led her to help other women who were scorned or lost in the world.

Honey was thick-hipped and bold in her stature. She enjoyed baking pies and mentoring young women the most. She wanted to pull young ladies out of their darkness, which she was far too familiar with. She found a safe space where she could acknowledge her past without welcoming it back to dim the light she worked so hard to stay in. That was the real reason why she dared not go in-depth about her stony, dark road.

Honey heard a knock on the door, so she turned the volume on the radio and switched her hips out of the kitchen. She greeted a young teen named Marcus, who rode his bike down her driveway and parked at the end of the steps.

"Hey, Ms. Honey," Marcus said, smiling and showing all his teeth. He licked his lips as if he tasted the pies from the outside. The sweet delicacy engulfed the air and flowed out of the doorway.

"Come on inside, Marcus," Honey said, closing the door swiftly. She did not want flies inside her home, buzzing around her pies. Honey would have had a fit.

Marcus followed his Godmother, Honey, towards the kitchen. The closer he got to the stove, his stomach growled.

"Those pies sure smell great!" Marcus complemented. He picked up three pieces of chocolate that were placed inside of a bowl on the kitchen table. He knew he was always welcome to any treats in Honey's home, so he didn't bother to ask. Asking his Godmother would be an insult.

"Of course, you can have some," Honey would say.

Marcus knew Honey too well, and he was protective of her.

"Don't you ruin your teeth," Honey said, watching him unravel the candy as he was careful not to touch the bare chocolate with his fingertips.

Honey took her soft brown hands, grabbed two of the pies, and placed them inside a decorated box.

"You should be careful carrying these pies, now," Honey warned. Her hand met her right hip and lightly rubbed his face. "Got a few hairs growing above that lip."

Honey had known Marcus since he was an infant. Now he was thirteen years old and had grown to be a young gentleman full of intellect and well-mannered.

"I will be careful, Ms. Honey. I'll fall and break my leg before I let one of these pies hit the ground," he joked.

When Marcus' mom told him to pick up the dessert, he gladly went to see Honey. It was an excuse in the world to be underneath her. Honey grew to be sweet like her name, and she spoiled Marcus rotten.

Marcus pulled out some money from his jeans pocket. "Here you go, Ms. Honey."

"What are you doing with that?" Honey asked.

"Please, take the money, Ms. Honey. My mom would be so upset if you didn't."

Honey took the money and quickly gave it back.

"I took it. Now, put that back in your pocket and hush your mouth," Honey warned.

"But, she will ask if you took the money."

Honey smiled. "I did. You saw me take the money, and I returned it."

She grabbed two boxed pies and stepped to the front door. "Here you go," Honey said, handing him the boxes. "Call me when you make it home."

"I will. Thank you, Ms. Honey. I love you!" he said before carefully biking out of the gate and onto the sidewalk.

Honey's phone rang, and she knew it was Maple before she answered it.

"Hey, girl," she answered.

"You mean to tell me she still doesn't know how to make her own damn pies yet," Maple said, laughing. "You got one for me?"

"Of course I do, and what are you doing besides being nosey?" Honey asked as she ran her dishwater to wash a few pans.

When Honey got on the phone with Maple, they might have called it a night because they would chat for hours.

"Nothing. I figured I finished watching the stories that I had recorded. I got to know when Mandy is going to figure out that she is being cheated on. I can't believe her husband is sleeping with her boss," Maple said, referring to the TV show they enjoyed.

"Clueless and crazy," Honey said. "Mandy is the definition of stupid."

Maple heard a startling noise across the street. She peeped out of her blinds. The fussing Maple heard distracted her from talking any further. Maple was quiet, and it was not like Maple to get quiet so suddenly.

"Are you there?" Honey asked.

"Speaking of stories. Girl, we got one going on right now," Maple said.

"What are you talking about, Maple?"

"Go to your bedroom window and look out. Hurry up. This is getting good," Maple said. "The young girl who moved in with the *married* man is getting kicked out of the house right now!"

Maple witnessed the aggressive man throw a bag over the rail of his porch.

"What a hot mess?" Honey said, moving the satin curtain and pulling down the blinds. "I knew that this day was coming."

Honey heard and witnessed her neighbors, Ivy and Brian, arguing on the front porch.

"I can't believe you are cheating on me," Ivy fussed, refusing to believe that Brain would turn against her. "All of the things we've been through, and this is how you do me?"

"I don't need a woman questioning me," Brian argued, shoving her luggage out the door. "Go ahead and leave!"

"Fine," she said, bending over and collecting her clothes. "Nothing good is ever going to happen to your sorry, black ass."

"I got a home, a pot to piss in, and a window to throw it out of, including you," Brian said as he pointed at her. He wiped his hands as if he had taken out the trash.

Brian showed no remorse for his distraught mistress, whom he lured into his home and whispered sweet lies to captivate her gullible heart. He had fun with her and was done having her around entirely.

"Ain't no woman going to tell me what to do," Brian said. "I thought you knew your place."

"You're such a damn coward!" Ivy yelled, clutching a few things in her hands.

Brian slammed the door shut and left Ivy to defend herself.

"Poor thing. Should we help?" Honey asked Maple as she watched Ivy standing in the yard looking hopeless.

"Girl, I'm going out there to get *all* the tea," Maple said, slipping on her pink, fuzzy shoes and hurried out of her house.

"Maple? Lord, have mercy. She's going out there," Honey said. Honey threw on her sweater and decided to join in. She wasn't going to allow Maple to meddle in the chaos alone, and she wanted to hear the story first-hand. Maple had tendencies to exaggerate the truth a little.

"Do you need any help, sweetie?" Maple asked, crossing the street.

"No, I don't need your help," Ivy said, too embarrassed to admit what had happened.

"I see. You're having a tough time. What's the matter?" Maple asked as if she didn't know what transpired or the backstory. "You left a pair of pantyhose in the bushes," she pointed.

"Is everything okay?" Honey asked, looking at Maple, who seemed eager to listen to how Ivy would explain her story.

Ivy had her things spread over the lawn, including a couple of garments on her shoulders. She refused to look at them in their eyes.

"Everything is fine," Ivy said.

"No, everything isn't," Maple said. "You moved in with a-

"Maple," Honey interrupted politely. "Please, let's just help the young woman." Honey picked up a pair of shoes that fell out of her half-opened luggage. "Nice shoes," Honey complimented, trying to make light of the situation.

"Thank you," Ivy said, wishing they both would leave.

"Do you have anywhere to go?" Maple asked. "Honey would be glad to take you in."

"Excuse me, Maple."

"I took the last poor woman in," Maple said, "and that heifer knew she wrecked my last nerves. But we got her on the straight and narrow. Now, this is your turn."

"Please, ladies, I am fine," Ivy said. She stuffed a shirt into a bag and tried not to curse them out as she continued picking up her clothes from the grass.

"Let's cut to the chase," Maple said, "you had an affair with that married man and moved in with him thinking it would be wonderful. You believed he was going to divorce his wife and marry you."

"But when he was done with you, he kicked you out—just like we thought he would," Honey said.

"It was just a matter of time," Maple replied, shaking her head. "I'm surprised it lasted this long."

"Nine months and three weeks," Honey said.

"You two are some nosey ass, old ass women," Ivy snapped.

"Nosey enough to look and kind enough to help," Maple said, "now, let's collect your things and try to get you together. It's about to rain."

When they got inside Honey's home, Honey handed them a slice of pie at the kitchen table.

"Yes, God, this pie still hit the spot!" Maple said, stomping her foot. "Make you want to hurt yourself."

"Thank you," Honey said, "are you going to eat?" Honey asked Ivy, who sat at the table with a long face.

Ivy began sobbing and pulling her curly black hair back.

Maple moved the plate, "Girl, don't you add no salt water to this pie."

"Ivy, poor thing. There are plenty of single men out there. You're beautiful, and everything will be fine," Honey said.

"Everybody makes mistakes," Maple said. "Nobody is perfect."

"I feel so stupid," Ivy said. She grabbed the tissue that Honey handed her and wiped her tears. "I'm so embarrassed."

"We all have a past," Honey said. "You got to move forward."

"Thanks for letting me stay for the night. I'll be headed out by tomorrow evening," Ivy said, then wept.

"That sounds like it hurts so bad," Maple said, rubbing Ivy's shoulder.

"What's the matter, now," Honey asked, grabbing Ivy's hand to console her.

"Who am I kidding? I have no place to go," Ivy said. "My family would look at me like a disgrace. I can't go back to North Carolina. My parents already see me as a nobody. They are going to be ashamed of me."

Honey was lost for words, so she tapped her fingernails on the table and looked at Maple.

"Excuse us for a minute," Maple said. "Let your tears flow as much as you need to," she told Ivy as she guided Honey to the far end of the kitchen.

They started semi-whispering amongst each other, not caring if Ivy heard them.

"Before I say yes, can we help her?" Honey asked. "The girl is an emotional wreck. You know I can't stand all of that crying."

"We helped plenty of young women to get on their feet. How hard could she be?" Maple asked.

Ivy cried harder, erupting tears along with a yell.

"Aw, shit," Maple said, then she asked Honey, "What would Ms. Sugar do?"

"Ms. Sugar would walk up to her and tell her to shut the hell up. But I can't do that now. But, as tough as we were, I'm pretty sure we can help if she wants it," Honey said.

"By the look of her pitiful self, she doesn't have much choice," Maple said.

TWO

Maple woke early and started working, stitching a dress for her niece, Tally. When she got tired of measuring and cutting the fabric, she picked up the phone to see how things were going with Honey.

"Is she still sleeping?" Maple asked.

"Yes, she's still sleeping," Honey said, "she cried all night long too."

Honey sat at her table and fixed her cup of tea. She wondered how much of a mess Ivy was in. "I think we have a lot of work to do. How's that dress coming along?" Honey asked.

"Girl, it's coming. I don't have enough material to cover her. She's thick like gumbo. Would I be wrong to charge extra?"

Honey laughed. "I'll be over to help you later on. I think I hear Ivy waking up. I'll call you back."

Honey got up and walked toward the guest bedroom she had prepared for Ivy. She tapped lightly on the door and saw her lying on her side with her eyes open.

"Did you sleep well," Honey asked.

"Yes, well, kind of," she said, "Thank you, Ms. Honey."

"No problem. I knew you had a rough time yesterday. Why don't you wash up and meet me in the kitchen?"

Ivy eased off the bed and opened the curtain to let the sunlight illuminate the room. She stretched her arms high and saw that Brian had given her a ring on her finger. Ivy slid it off and looked at it before entering the bathroom to freshen up. She took the diamond ring and flushed it. At that moment, she did not want anything to do with him.

"Go to hell, Brian," she whispered.

Ivy was more upset to believe she was worthy enough to be his wife. Her flawless cocoa butter skin and slim waist were insufficient to keep him. Not to mention the mind-blowing sex and waiting on him hand and foot. She thought she had done everything right to lure a man away from his vows.

"How did I get here?" Ivy asked herself. She was certainly not raised to be so foolish.

She was glad that a stranger, Honey, was kind enough to take her in and treat her well without judgment.

After she showered, she was met with love in the form of a hot meal.

"Are you hungry?" Honey asked. She gestured for Ivy to come and eat, giving her no option to say no. "Say grace," Honey said politely.

"Lord, thank you for this food, and please bless Ms. Honey, who prepared it," she said, smiling a little. She took her fork and dug into her eggs. "Thank you, Ms. Honey."

"You can stop thanking me. I'm glad to help you get back on your feet," Honey said, enjoying her biscuit. "Care for some jelly?"

"I'll take some," Ivy said, "hopefully, I won't be in your way for too long."

"Do you have a plan?"

Ivy looked down at her half-eaten biscuit and teared up.

Honey grabbed her face quickly before a tear dropped and said, "Oh, no, baby. You better not cry. You cried your last tear last night over that sorry ass man," Honey snapped. "Time for you to embrace your new journey and a brand new start. Consider yourself blessed, do you hear me?" she asked.

"Yes, ma'am."

"Good. Now, I'm going to ask you to do some things. Don't question me; just do it. First thing first, what do you like to do?"

"I don't know."

"Do you know how to cook?"

"A little."

"What's a little?"

"Umm-

"Don't worry about it, baby." Honey took her dish and placed it in the sink. "Starting tomorrow, I'm going to teach you what you need to know about being a grown woman and it's way more than being in the kitchen and looking cute. No disrespect towards your mama. Sometimes, young girls are hard headed. Let me show you how a real woman struts herself."

Honey twitched her hips, slowly eased down on her seat, and crossed her legs.

"Okay, Ms. Honey!" Ivy said, impressed, "Who taught you that?"

"Years of experience," Honey said as she sipped her coffee. "Your season is about to change. God allowed you to come into my and Maple's life for a good reason."

After a much-needed conversation with Honey, Ivy decided to feel the breeze and go outdoors, knowing that Brian would be outside, too. She sat on Honey's porch, sipping lemonade and pretending she did not notice him.

Brian was in the sun, half-naked, showing his well-defined abs and back muscles. The sunlight glistened on his caramel skin as he washed his black Jeep.

Ivy envisioned herself jumping on top of him while he was hot and sweaty and doing all the fun sexual activities they used to do. It did not matter where they were; they had a high for making love in public places. The thrill of getting caught turned them on even more.

Ivy snapped the fantasy out of her mind right before Brian saw her leaning on the rail. Looking in the opposite direction, she acted like she was not paying him any attention.

"So, you haven't had enough of me," Brian yelled across the fence. He pumped his chest muscles and winked at Ivy. "It's not polite to be stalking people."

"I'm not stalking you. I had better before. Who do you think you are?" Ivy asked.

"Ivy, I know you miss me."

"Boy, please. I'm moving on to better things, and you're going to wish I stayed."

Brian laughed. "I bet you are moving on with another man who will make the same mistake as I did. Look at you, staying at Ms. Honey's house because you had nowhere else to go." He grinned.

"I can't wait for karma to come and bite you in your ass. I wasn't the only one wrong in the relationship. You know two wrongs don't make a right. You are married, and you broke *your* vows."

Honey heard the commotion and stepped outside.

"Excuse me," Honey said, looking at Ivy. She knew she did not need to talk to Brian unless she missed him.

"I'm sorry for my yelling, Ms. Honey," Brian apologized.

"He talked to me first," Ivy said, then she entered the house.

"Brian, you ignore her and worry about that divorce before you go around breaking women's hearts," Honey said. Honey walked inside of her home and shut her door. "Ivy, what in the hell is wrong with you?"

"I'm sorry, Ms. Honey. I shouldn't have entertained him," Ivy said. She sat on the couch and leaned back. "I want to kill his ass," she whispered.

Honey hurried into the kitchen, pulled out a butcher knife, and said, "Go and do it! Lure him back in and stab him straight in the heart, but I suggest you aim for the neck first."

Ivy looked shocked at Honey's reaction.

"C'mon and grab it, or do you want to blow his brains out?" Honey asked seriously. When she called out Ivy's bluff, she continued, "Ivy, you knew that man was married."

"He said that it was over."

"And the Devil is the father of lies."

"I should have known. All of my life, I have been lied to. I got foolish in the head and-

"We all made mistakes. I made many of them, but I learned, and I grew. And I am damn proud of the woman that I became."

"Ms. Honey, what kind of mistakes have you made?" Ivy asked seriously. Ivy denied believing that Ms. Honey did not have a perfect life or a righteous upbringing in how she carried herself.

"You think I've been baking pies and watching stories all my life. Child, I saw some things and did some things that would make you look like a saint."

"Like what?"

"Come, follow me," Honey said.

They went into Honey's bedroom, where Honey pulled out an old picture of herself.

"Ms. Honey, this is you?" Ivy asked, staring at the photo of Honey in her early twenties. Honey was wearing bell bottoms and a crop top. "Your afro was everything!"

"Tell me about it." Honey smiled.

"You were a fine woman," Ivy said. "I never would have guessed-

"Excuse me? I'm *still* fine, baby. And sugar, if I wanted Brian, I could get him. I'd rock his world and have him sleeping with his thumb in his mouth," Honey said, placing her hand on her hips.

"Ms. Honey," Ivy said, "I didn't know you could talk like that."

"Looks can be very deceiving, Ivy. In that picture, I was depressed and bitter as hell."

"Why? You look so happy."

` "Life took a major toll on me, and I thought I would never see my way out. I became addicted to the streets."

Ivy eased the picture down and was stunned at Honey's confession.

"That's why I don't judge people and their journeys. We all have a pathway to the promise. I prayed for you when I saw you walk into Brian's house. Maple and I both knew that this day would come." Honey sat next to Ivy and continued, "It seemed like ever since I walked out of misery, my calling was to help women see the best in themselves." Honey lifted Ivy up and led her to a long mirror in the corner of the bedroom. "Tell me, what do you see?"

Ivy despised that question.

"Be honest," Honey whispered. "This is a safe place."

"Guilt, ashamed, brokenness...abandonment, hurt... a disgrace," Ivy said, crying.

"Oh, but a change will come when you get ready to leave here."

THREE

"My dress is so gorgeous," Tally said, admiring the long, violet dress that wrapped perfectly around her curves. "You did a fantastic job, Ms. Maple."

"Thank you," Maple said, smirking at Tally. She saw that the dress reflected well on her dark skin. Maple's hard work in designing the perfect style paid off. The cursing and praying were worth every thread she sewed, trying to please her customer.

"I hardly want to take this off. I am going to be the queen of the ball," Tally said. She eased off the stool, twirled around, and grabbed her purse. Then, she handed Maple the money she owed her.

Maple counted the money and stuffed it in her bra. "Paid me extra. That's why you're my favorite client."

"Well, I know I was difficult to deal with. My perfection and all my-

"Ass," Maple joked. "I'm glad you love it. Now, let me help you take it off." Maple unzipped the back of the dress and noticed a bruise on her upper back. "Tally, I know you're black, but you ain't that damn black. Why do I see a bruise?"

Shocked, Tally tried to play it off, but Maple wasn't trying to hear the excuse she had to say. After the second fight, Tally went back to be with her abuser, and the situation got physical again. Tally looked down and was frightened to see Maple's face. She knew her cousin, Maple, was sick and tired of the games and lies.

"You're still fooling with that man. Keep it up, and I will be making a dress for your funeral," Maple said.

Maple was pissed.

"No, Ms. Maple. I left that man. This happened a while ago. I had no idea I had a bruise," she said sadly. "You have to believe me."

Maple sat quietly on the living room sofa and wished to believe that Tally had told her the truth. If she had known Tally was back dealing with her ex-boyfriend, Russell, she would have ripped that dress apart and demanded that she get therapy.

"Okay, Tally. I pray to God that you are telling me the truth. If you are not, God will reveal it to me."

"Oh, I know," she said, putting on her t-shirt. "Well, that's the first dress."

"Why do you need another dress?"

"This is the one that I wear at the beginning of the event, and the second dress is the one where I can dance in," she said, swaying her hips, trying to lighten the mood.

"Okay, fine. I'll design another one."

"Thanks so much!" She squeezed Maple and kissed her on the cheek. "I'm going to be the baddest woman there!"

"Yes, you are. Tally," Maple said softly. "Promise me that you left that man for good."

"I promise. And I'm sorry that-

"No need to apologize to me. Why do you need to tell me you're sorry?" Maple asked angrily. "I'm not the one beating your ass! I pour everything into my family, and they won't listen. What good is it for me to help broken women out on the street, but my own flesh and blood is driving me up the wall? Doing things you have no business doing as if I know nothing about living a dangerous life." Maple reached into her bra, snatched the money out, and laid the cash on the coffee table. She placed the dress across her arms.

"What are you doing?" Tally asked.

"Until you prove that you left that man alone, I will not approve of you wearing anything I made. Do I make myself clear?" Maple asked.

"No offense, but I am nothing like your daughter. I made an honest mistake. He promised me that he would never hit me again. I admit I was stupid for going back, but you can trust me." Tally said.

"You can have the dress *if* you're still alive," Maple snapped. "I care more about your well-being than you looking stunning at a ball. And as far as my daughter is concerned, she started off like *you!* You're going down the same path, and it's a hard, rocky road, Tally. If I give you this dress, it would mean that I'm okay with you dressing up in your pain."

"Ms. Maple, I am completely done with Russell. I know my worth now."

"Good. That means you will have no problem walking away. I'm sure I won't hear anything about you and Russell in the next few months."

"No, you won't. I promise."

"Your dress will be waiting for you. I ain't changing my mind."

Once Tally left, Maple grabbed the phone and called Honey.

"Honey, I had a strange feeling that if I gave Tally that dress, I wouldn't see her again."

"That wasn't a strange feeling," Honey said, assuring her that she trusted her gut and made the right decision.

"I'm getting so frustrated and tired. Between Tally and my daughter Jasmine, I'm running out of hope."

"We will never give up on them, and I mean *never*," Honey said.

FOUR

"Everything is fine. Trust me," Ivy said, speaking with her mother, Nora. "No, Mama, you don't have to come here. I'll see you soon. I love you."

"You ought to be ashamed of yourself for lying to your mother," Honey said, walking past the bedroom.

"Ms. Honey, I don't think you would understand. If I told my family the truth, they would think that I was a failure," Ivy said, crossing her arms. "All I need is enough time to get on my feet and tell my family that my relationship with Brain didn't work out."

"Is that really the plan," Honey said.

"Yes, unless you have a better one," she said, smirking.

"Even though I am against people lying to their parents. I'll show you mercy," Honey said. She peeked into the corner and saw the Bible under some folded laundry. "Have you been reading that Bible I gave you?" she asked, knowing she hadn't.

"I tried," Ivy said, "but there's a lot in there that I don't understand. But I know God is real because you and Maple are women who are Heaven-sent." She smiled.

"Come on to the kitchen. I'll show you how to make biscuits."

"Is that all you do is cook?"

"Well, it's good for me. It is quite relaxing. Come on, it's going to be fun."

"If you say so, Ms. Honey."

Honey and Ivy laughed a lot, as if they knew each other far more than they had in the week they spent together. Ivy was more like the daughter she never had. Honey couldn't focus on it, but Ivy was unique and easy to love.

Ivy bit into her food and said, "Between all your food and your pies, I'm going to be as big as this house," she said, then giggled.

"You have a mighty long way to go," Honey replied.

"You think if I was bigger, maybe Brian would have wanted me?" Ivy asked, looking down at her slim figure.

"Brian is a boy, and boys don't know what they want. Ivy, you are beautiful the way you are, and until you recognize that, you won't be happy," Honey said.

Ivy tried working on her self-esteem, but it came too slowly. In the mornings, she started washing her face and brushing her teeth with her eyes closed. Brian damaged her, and it destroyed her more, knowing that she gave him permission to do it. She went from spending hours admiring herself in the mirror to barely wanting to see her reflection.

"Ms. Honey, I want to know more about you and your story," she asked softly.

"Why do you want to know that?" Honey asked, watching Ivy collect and place the dishes in the sink. Honey felt like she shared enough.

"I told you everything about me in the past few days," Ivy said, "it's only fair because when I talked to you last night, I realized something about me that I never knew. It helped me in some ways. My story showed me why I made bad decisions and acted like I do."

Honey sat quietly for a few seconds and battled her thoughts. On one hand, she had a pleasant life, but on the other, it was filled with too much sorrow. Honey didn't know the last time she had gone into details about what she had overcome. She tapped her nails at the table and was scared of confronting the demons she thought were dead. She dared not mention the names of some people she encountered.

"C'mon, Ms. Honey, please," Ivy begged.

Honey sat in silence and considered sharing her personal journey. She thought maybe Ivy had a point.

"Go pour us some coffee and listen, I'm *only* telling you."

"Thank you, Ms. Honey," Ivy said, wrapping her arms around Honey's shoulders.

"I don't even know where to begin," Honey said. She tried to think of how to ease the story to Ivy.

"When you were a child," Ivy said, sitting across the kitchen table and prepared to listen as if she were a classroom student.

"A child?" Honey questioned. "I guess so."

Honey sat down opposite of Ivy and grabbed her coffee mug. Honey's face looked as though she was in a twilight zone. Her memory zapped her back to her childhood of innocence, which later landed in chaos that robbed her of her sanity. She fought damn hard to redeem herself.

She saw herself dancing around with her favorite doll in the living room and not having a care in the world at the age of eight. She was full of light, yet trouble was brewing like a whirlwind and turned her world completely upside down. She opened her eyes and thought she was ready to go back and dig up the troublesome past that was buried. She tried to tell her story without cracking, but her emotions got the best of her.

"When I was eight years old, my mama. My mama's name...my mama' name was...she was...excuse me." Honey's voice trembled while she fought tears.

Honey got up from the table and entered the nearby bathroom, realizing she didn't even have the strength to speak about her late mom. She missed her so dearly. She wondered how in the world could she find the willingness to continue? Even at the bare mention of her mom, it gave her an indescribable emotional pain. She wept over the sink.

Ivy knocked softly on the bathroom door.

"I'm sorry, Ms. Honey. You don't have to tell your story. I apologize. I had no idea-

"You're fine, Ivy. Don't feel bad. I must do this."

Ivy waited ten minutes or so before Honey walked back inside the kitchen. Honey sipped her hot beverage, which was far too sweet. It tasted the same way her mother enjoyed her coffee.

Once Honey gathered herself together, She took one solid breath and spoke.

"I was born in Detroit, Michigan. Me, along with my older sister, Erica. My mother, my mother's name was Dessie," Honey said, smiling, then sipped her coffee.

"Was she a great cook?"

"Was she? Baby, where do you think I got it from? Hush, and let me tell my story," Honey said, laughing.

"One day, Mama went to a church convention, met a man, and fell in love, so they say. He was tall and broad and appeared to be very gentle. His name was Robert Morgan, and he was from Alabama. My sister and I thought the world of him for how he made Mama so happy. He would travel back and forth for two years to be with Mama. Then, he asked Mama to marry him one day, but we had to move to Alabama. Since we liked Mr. Morgan and wanted Mama to be happy, we said, 'Yes,' Honey said, smiling as she recalled the joy on her mama's face when they approved of the marriage.

Birmingham, Alabama 1963—-

"Come on, girls, we got to get ready for church," Dessie said. "Robert is already there, and we're running a bit late." Dessie fussed a little. "Stop all that griping, Clara."

"Erica is sick," I said, leaning on the wall in my yellow dress. I had tried that 'I don't feel good' trick too many times, and it always failed. Mama thought I persuaded Erica to pretend, too, so she politely scooted me out of the way to make sure I wasn't telling a fib.

"Erica, c'mon and get up," Dessie said, opening the bedroom door. She saw Erica was gravely ill with red eyes. Dessie knew she wasn't playing. "Lord, have mercy." She touched her hot forehead and her warm cheeks.

"I woke up feeling really bad," Erica whispered.

"I'mma have to give you some medicine and get you to the doctor in the morning," Dessie said. "Move back, I don't need you to get sick too, Clara," she told me.

I stood at the doorway and watched my sister suffering from a fever. She took slow, deep breaths and wheezed before she slumped her head back on her pillow.

"Sister, you're not joking, are you?" I asked. The small amount of hope I had wished she would tell me yes, but her illness was serious. I was terrified of how miserable she was.

Mama rushed back in with a spoon and some red liquid medicine. "Go to your room, Clara," Mama demanded.

But I was hard-headed and didn't want to move. I felt so sorry for her, and I watched how slowly she raised her head off the pillow. The simple gesture took all of her might to get up.

The phone rang, so Mama rushed into the kitchen to answer it.

"No, we are not going to make it to the church today. Erica is so sick," Dessie said.

"Good," Mr. Morgan said. I heard his deep voice tremble, "Dessie...they bombed the church."

"What?" Dessie screamed. "Who are they? Who would do such a thing?"

"Dessie...them white folks. The white folks would do such a thing," Mr. Morgan said.

"Lord, have mercy. Lord, have mercy, now! Is everybody okay-

The sirens in the background were loud, and the chaos from people accompanied the noise.

"...Four little girls were killed in the basement. Dessie, it's a mad house here. It's like a war. We are hurting really bad now. Hug the girls for me, and I'll try to be home as soon as possible."

Mama hung up the phone, startled at the news. She looked at me and pulled me into her chest, squeezing me.

"I'm so sorry. Mama brought you both down here because I wanted to get married, but if you or Erica want to leave, we will go," Mama said, tearing up. "We'll go without any hesitation, just say the word."

I didn't say anything. I was too shaken at what happened. I wasn't in Birmingham long, but I imagined that one day we could have been friends with those girls, but hatred took away that chance.

Once Mama released me, I left her crying in the living room. She asked God if we should go for good and what to do. The terrifying thought came across her mind that it could have easily been her daughters.

I wept for them. It wasn't fair.

I went into my sister's bedroom and lay across the foot of the bed while she lay asleep. I didn't care if I had gotten sick or not. I needed her. She was the only friend I had.

"I'm so sorry to hear that," Ivy said.

"I am, too, but I'm just getting started," Honey said.

FIVE

One afternoon, Maple was hoarded by fabrics in her living room. As she was sewing, her phone rang.

"Hello," she answered. There was so much noise in the background she barely heard the person on the other end. She said, "Hello," loudly.

"Hey, Mama."

"Jasmine, how are you?" Maple asked. It had been a month since she heard from her daughter, and she was elated to listen to her voice.

"I'm good, just here," Jasmine said.

"Where are you?"

"I'm out and I'm good. I need a small favor. I still have my card, and I need some money."

"Why don't you come and get it?" Maple asked nicely. She wished to see Jasmine.

"I ain't coming over there because I need money to get there," Jasmine said. She was irritated.

"You promise that you will come if-

"Just give me the money! I need it. It's the least you can do."

"Jas-

"Money!" Jasmine hung up the phone.

Maple threw the fabric down and decided to give it a break. Her spirit was broken. If only she knew where Jasmine was, she would go see her. It had been years since Maple had been on the streets, but she would quickly turn back if necessary.

Maple heard a knock on her front door and told Ivy to come in.

"Ms. Maple," Ivy said, holding fabrics in her hand. "I hope I got the right kind you asked for," Ivy said, seeing that Maple looked distraught. "Is everything okay?"

"Yes, everything is fine." She saw the materials that Ivy had purchased. "You did a good job."

"Ms. Maple, you are extremely talented. Have you thought about having your own store?" Ivy asked, looking around at the clutter. Maple had a few dresses hanging on the room's left side.

"With what money? I am good enough to work here."

Ivy figured she needed more space but decided to shut her mouth and mind her business. Maple was much more feisty than Honey.

Maple repeatedly rubbed her fingers across the same red fabric and stared into space.

Ivy looked to her right and saw a black and white photo of an older couple placed on the dresser.

"Who are these people?" Ivy asked.

Maple faced her and proudly announced, "That's my Mama. Her name was Ethel, and she was with my Grandpa John. Well, she was really my grandmother, but she raised me. My brother Leon and I called her Mama. Grandpa was a World War II Veteran who came back from the war when they took that picture. That's why Mama was so happy, but I never got a chance to get to know him. You heard of the Tuskegee Airman, right?" She moved her gray and black hair from her face to show her wide, small.

"Of course," Ivy lied.

"He was one of them. And Mama stood by his side until the day he died, then she moved up here. I am proud to say that I'm a product of her. I'm just a little rougher around the edges, but she's why I love doing this," Maple said, looking at the clothing she worked on. "I don't know how she did that same thing as me and kept a neat house."

"Well, I would love to-.

"Hear my story," Maple said, then laughed. "Honey told me how you suckered her into knowing her business." She laid her hands on her hips. "I tell you what. I'll tell you about my life, but I am not responsible for the words coming out of my mouth. Do you understand me?"

"I do," Ivy said.

"I was six years old—

Detroit, Michigan, 1960

"Why are you riding your bike in your good skirt?" Mama asked me.

"I'm sorry, Mama. I didn't want to wait until my pants were dry," I said sadly, looking at my favorite green dress I ruined, along with a scraped left knee. I fell against the concrete, racing against the other neighborhood kids.

I knew Mama was going to scold me. Instead, she lifted my head with her long hands and said, "Don't worry, I can fix it."

"You can?" I asked.

"Yes, God gifted me. Now, take it off and hand it to me. I'll stitch it up in no time. Maybe you learned your lesson." She smiled and took a bandage from the dresser drawer.

Mama was sweet and upright. She was barely caught in a foul mood unless someone picked on her children, which rarely happened. Mama was my doctor, school teacher, friend.... everything.

"But don't make me a God," Mama would say, "Never depend on anyone but Him," she preached.

I took off my dress, put on some dry clothes, and headed to the kitchen when my brother Leon walked in. He was twelve years old, bony, and straight up and down.

"Hey, Mama," Leon said.

"Don't hey me. What were you doing when you didn't see your sister fall off her bike?"

"Ummm," Leon said.

"Playing with Clarissa," I said, teasing him about his girlfriend.

"If you keep messing with that girl, you're going to find yourself in a world of trouble," Mama said.

"I thought that was only white girls," Leon joked.

He joined me at the table.

Mama paid him no mind. She welcomed his charming ways as long as he didn't smart-mouth her, which he knew better.

Although we didn't grow up with a typical mom and dad, it never felt like it. Mama Ethel had enough love to cover the neighborhood. If anyone got too comfortable and called her Mama, we got upset. Leon and I wanted Mama all to ourselves.

Mom's joyous crackle and kindness drew everyone into our home, even Oscar. Oscar was unkempt and often wandered the streets, speaking loudly to himself and pointing at things that nobody saw but him.

The kids and I in the neighborhood would run and hide behind anything big enough when he came strolling down the street like a drunken man. I would peek behind the bushes until he was far gone before I started playing in the yard again.

We would often hear Oscar before we saw him staggering closer to our home. He was around Mama's age but aged terribly with droopy eyes. No matter the weather, he wore stained jeans and the same brown baseball cap.

Often, Mama met him in the yard and invited him inside to get cleaned up. He'd take a shower, and we would hear him shout, "I'm a Black Flier! We fight, we fight!"

After he was done washing up, Mama handed him clean clothes and a pair of Leon's socks.

Leon griped.

Mama told him to hush up because it wasn't like he paid for it.

After Oscar showered, he left black stains in the tub. When he left, Mama would get on her knees and scrub it back clean as she hummed her favorite gospel melodies. Not once did she complain, and not once did Mama shame Oscar. She treated him as if he were family.

"It's time for you to eat," Ethel said to Oscar.

Oscar almost looked like a new man with his clean-shaven face when he sat at the table with us, but Leon kept a pocket knife in case he got irate. Oscar never acted out in front of Mama. He kept his composure and held decent conversations. A few bread crumbs sprinkled his chest while he ate, and he would take the back of his hand and wipe the crumbs off his mouth, and the crumbs fell onto the floor.

Mama never got upset over the mess. Mama made Oscar feel safe. Mama made him feel human.

"Why do you keep letting him in here?" Leon asked, upset.

It was the next day at the kitchen table, and it was an answer that I wanted to know, too. Mama always went the extra mile to help people even when we needed help.

"We are all God's children," Mama said, "Now, let's eat. Say grace, Anna. Your brother is too mean and his spirit isn't good right now," Mama said.

After I said the grace, we dug into our potatoes, green beans, and fried chicken. I was so hungry that I began to eat like Oscar did, wiping my mouth with the back of my hand. Mama made the best fried chicken.

"We didn't get any mail today," I said, breaking the silence.

"Mail," Leon said, stopping mid-bite of his food. "What are you doing checking the mail? Checking the mail is *my* job," he fussed.

"Leon," Mama said sternly.

"What's wrong with me checking the mail?" I asked.

I thought I was helping out since I was only old enough to do so much around the house. I swept, mopped, and fixed my bed, but I wanted to help as much as possible.

"Little girls should not be in the mailbox. Anything can jump out of that box. Spiders, lizards, frogs! One time, a girl put her hand in the box and-

"Leon," Mama called his name, but he kept scaring me.

"Her hand got bit and it turned purple and molded into black and yellow. Then slime ran down her arms, and they had to cut it off!"

"Nooo!" I screamed.

"Leon!" Mama slapped the table, "Anna, go make your bed. We have some errands to run."

I gladly left the table and shook off the gruesome image that my brother planted inside of my head. I hated bugs.

"I'm sorry, Mama," Leon said.

"How long will you keep it a secret? Anna needs to know," Mama whispered.

"She's too young. I can't imagine how she'd feel if she found out. It's already hard enough that I must take care of her," Leon said.

"And what do you think I'm doing? Twirling my thumbs all day. And for the record, I would rather you enjoy your life and be a young man. I don't need help if that's what you think. When your grandpa served in the war, I had four kids running around." She smirked.

"But... you're old now," Leon said in the sweetest way possible.

"But I don't feel old," Mama said, giggling at Leon, trying not to hurt her feelings. "But because you're almost an adult, I chose to respect your wishes. Just please know the day has to come for you to tell her."

"Bed is made up," I said, walking back into the kitchen.

"Good. We have to pick you out a dress and buy Leon a tie."

"And some socks," Leon joked, "and a green tie. I want a green tie."

"You're going to get whatever color tie I can afford," Mama said, snuggling his black right cheek. "Now, when we're gone, you better not bring any girls into this house."

"What if I bring her in so she can do the dishes?" Leon asked.

I laughed at Mama's reaction. She took the back of her hand and smacked him lightly on the head. Mama called it a love tap.

In the middle of our laughter, we heard a helicopter. It sounded like it was flying lower than usual. Then, suddenly, a giant rock smashed into our front window. We ducked as glass crashed everywhere in the living room. I scooted under the table as Leon bravely looked out and saw that Oscar had thrown the rock.

"Take cover! Take cover!" Oscar shouted as the neighbors stepped outside and saw him jumping around and warning everyone to get down. Oscar was flapping his arms frantically as he continued to yell and run in a circle.

"You crazy motherfucker!" Leon screamed, "You could have hurt my mom and my sister!"

"Hush your mouth, Leon," Mama scolded him. "Oscar!" She called his name. "Calm down, right now. Do you hear me?" She slowly approached him and spoke gently, "We are all safe, and nobody is going to hurt you. Look at what you did to my house."

Oscar's face changed from an irate man to someone showered with compassion. He fell to his knees and started crying, realizing the damage he had done to Mama's house.

"I'm so sorry... I'm so sorry... I'll fix it. I'll-

"Don't worry about it. Are you hungry?" Mama asked.

Leon and I looked at Mama strangely while she rubbed Oscar's shoulder.

Shattered glass all over the living room floor, and she wanted to feed him? Our next-door neighbors, The Thompsons, shook their heads in anger and went back into their house. They were more upset than Mama was, and they felt like he was undeserving of being fed after the damage he caused.

I agreed.

"Anna, scoop up some mashed potatoes and give him a nice piece of fried chicken," Mama said. "No scraps."

I quickly fixed Oscar a plate and rushed it to Mama. I wanted him to hurry out of our yard in case he had another fit.

Mama handed him the plate and smiled, "Next time, you don't throw any bombs. You just take cover."

We saw Oscar leave while he ate the mashed potatoes with his hands, ignoring the fork.

A few days later, poor Oscar was killed. He wandered into someone's yard and started beating on the door. The man didn't know how to deal with him, so he shot poor Oscar.

I cried and was hurt far more than I expected to.

My mama was the only one I saw that treated him nicely. I asked her why she was so kind to him, and she said, "He served in the war, along with your grandpa. The same country he fought for turned their backs. Have mercy on others because you never know what people may face."

SIX

"Brian, what do you want?" Honey asked, opening the door. She saw he held a basket full of garments.

"Ivy left some things, and I figured I'd fold them up and give them to her," he said. "Because I'm such a gentleman." He handed Honey the basket and smirked.

"Brian, you're a whore and you can't keep playing around," Honey said. "What about your wife?"

"I love her. We spent time apart, but now it's time to amend our relationship—for better or for worse, right? Tell Ivy, I said that I thank her for everything, and hopefully, my wife loves all the new tricks she taught me."

"Goodbye, Brian," Honey said, shutting the door.

"Who was that?" Ivy asked.

"Take a wild guess," Honey said, handing her the clothes.

"That asshole," she said.

When Ivy was alone in her bedroom, she scanned through her clothes and took out a red pair of lingerie. She pressed it against her body. She thought that when he saw me in this, he was going to keep me. But dressing sexy was not enough. She believed she was over Brian, but going so long without intimacy was not normal for her. She thought it would be too odd to take the shower head and please herself in Honey's house. She had to ask herself if she wanted to change for the good or find a new man she could lay under.

"Are you okay, Ivy?" Honey asked.

"Yes, I'm fine."

"Okay, Ivy. Don't let that bastard win."

Later that day, Honey and Ivy sat on the back porch to chat, and Honey continued to tell her story.

Mama had two sisters. The oldest was Gayle and the youngest was Sweetie. They visited the South to spend their first holiday with us in Birmingham. Erica and I anticipated them every hour and couldn't wait to see their faces. Mama was in the kitchen preparing meals and over-cleaning the

house. She had to make sure it was spotless.

My Aunt Gayle was spunky and bold with a carefree attitude. Aunt Gayle was also a sharp dresser and shared the same brown skin tone as Mama. My baby auntie was witty. She had brighter skin and took after my great-grandmother's look. All three had fluffy hair, but Mama's hair was longer. Regarding personality, I was more like Mama and Aunt Sweetie because Aunt Gayle would jump mean sometimes out of the blue, and then she apologized later as if nothing happened.

I saw them pull up in the driveway in Aunt Sweetie's yellow Cadillac.

"They're here!" I shouted, running outside and hugging Aunt Sweetie first.

Mama came out and greeted her sisters, and they smiled, which would light up the darkest places. They jumped around in the yard in a circle, holding hands like children at a picnic. It was so cute to see. Erica and I took the luggage from the car and paraded in the house.

"Girl, this house is nice," Sweetie said, admiring the brick and brown two-story house. "Negros, ain't doing as bad as I thought down here."

"That southern man is treating you well," Gayle said, admiring the living room and rubbing her hand on the leather sofa.

"Come on, take off your coats, and settle down," Dessie said, holding Gayle's coat. "Is this real fur?"

"Fake stuff makes my skin itch," Gayle said, sitting on the sofa.

"Since when? We all grew up piss poor," Sweetie said. "And none of your hand-me-downs were regal," Sweetie mocked her fancy manners before she hung her coat and sat herself down.

It wasn't long before they were settled at the round kitchen table, talking and laughing like they hadn't seen each other in years. They each had hot cups of tea placed in front of them. I sat in the living room and admired them like they were superstars. I hoped I would grow up as pretty as they were.

"How are the men down here?" Sweetie asked. "Do they greet you with a kiss on your hand? Maybe they take their hats off to say, 'How do you do?' But, I bet their breaths smell like hot water cornbread."

"They got to be something special. He got my sister moving down here in bombingham," Gayle teased with her arm leaning on the back of the chair. Sometimes, Gayle acted a little manly.

"Well, I'm glad my sisters came to see me," Dessie said.

I still believed Mama had a little guilt left over for moving us away from the North. Racism was everywhere, but Alabama and Mississippi played tug of war to see who would be the most evil.

"We almost didn't make it," Gayle said, looking at Sweetie, "We got pulled over by a pig in Tennessee, and Sweetie smart-mouthed the man."

"He wasn't going to talk to me crazy or in any kind of way. He saw two colored women driving clean, and he got the nerve to pull us over and ask where we were going," Sweetie said.

"Sweetie said none of your damn business. I thought for sure we were going to be killed," Gayle said.

"We were tired, and I had to pee," Sweetie said.

"It turned out that he was kind of nice," Gayle said. "Told us to watch our speed and make sure we stopped at the colored stations only like we were ignorant to the bullshit."

"Which was another twelve miles," Sweetie added, rolling her eyes, "but anything to see our sister, Dessie."

"It was only God who had mercy," Dessie said. She was so disappointed in Sweetie's behavior.

"Do I hear my other two favorite girls?" Mr. Morgan asked, parading into the house.

"What do you say?" Gayle asked playfully.

Mr. Morgan took his hat off, hugged them, and welcomed my aunties into the home. He chuckled and joked a lot with them.

Mama eyed a small bottle of scotch from his coat pocket and knew he had been drinking, but it wasn't anything to be concerned about. He remained a gentle giant.

"I'm ready to whoop your ass in cards," Gayle said.

"Gayle, why the hell are you cursing in front of the deacon?" Sweetie asked.

"Hell, as long as he's not the bishop," Gayle said. "Besides, we are about to be family soon. It's the holidays, and we have a wedding to plan."

"And we are not changing for nobody," Sweetie said. "Cheers to our future brother-in-law. Domm, da, da dom," Sweetie sang, raising her glass.

"You sound like you've been fooling around in my cabinet," Mr. Morgan joked. He opened the cabinet door and showed all the liquor he had brought. Three rows of bottles of different kinds of liquor filled the cabinet shelves.

"Damn, deacon," Gayle said. "Dessie, you didn't tell me this man got his own liquor store."

Later that night, Mama had a conversation with Mr. Morgan.

"What's going on?" Dessie asked.

"What do you mean, Dessie?" Mr. Morgan asked. He felt he knew what she was talking about.

"You and your drinking," Dessie said. She saw the look of frustration in his eyes. "I don't mind you drinking. I don't want it to become a problem."

It was apparent that the bombing of 16th Street Baptist Church started to weigh heavy on him. Mr. Morgan was sensitive and cared for everyone like family. He never met a stranger.

"Dessie...," he said, taking a slow, deep breath. "I'm a Black man in America who's responsible for you and two Black girls. I heard the stories and saw the scars, but this time, I was there to witness it all for myself, how we mean nothing in this world. I thought I was strong enough to protect them, but after the tragic murder of four young girls who look just like Erica and Clara and the white thugs who got away with it... I don't know. I don't know if I can give them what they need in this white man's world." He slapped the back of his right hand to his open left palm.

"No man ever loved me the way that you do. When I told you I had two girls, you welcomed my babies in your arms and into your heart. Just know that if God allowed something to happen to any of us, you did enough," Dessie said.

Honey's story was interrupted by a knock on the front door.

"That's my Godson coming to get those pies to carry," Honey said.

"Mr. Morgan sounded like a great man," Ivy said.

"Well, hold on to that thought."

SEVEN

"Ms. Maple, it seems like you're dressing every woman in the city for the ball,"

Ivy said, admiring all the gowns Maple was putting together.

Ivy came over to Maple's house and decided to tell her the news that she had a job interview. But, somehow, she stayed longer than she expected. She became in awe of Maple's work.

"What do you think about this?" Maple asked, "Do young girls like this style?"

Maple rubbed Tally's dress and wondered if Tally was doing well or remained in that violent relationship. She hung the dress up and decided to take a much-needed break.

"I like seeing smiles on faces," Maple said.

"I hope I find purpose in life," Ivy said.

"You're still young. When I was your age, I was so lost," Maple said, hanging more dresses in the closet.

"But your mama, she was so sweet," Ivy said.

Ivy thought, with Maple's upbringing and good roots, that she would be exempt from facing a hard life, but Maple reminded her that it didn't mean a damn thing as long as the Devil was working.

After a while, Maple poured them a glass of iced tea and continued her story...

"Thank you for fixing my window, Mr. Bill," Mama said.

"No problem. I don't mind it all. You're such a sweet lady. The way you treated Oscar, I know there's a God in you," Bill, the old man said, picking up his tools from the floor.

"It's my pleasure to do right in the eyes of God," Mama smiled, handing him the money.

"Is that your granddaughter over there?" he asked, placing his blue hat on his gray head.

I was a little girl sitting in the corner of the living room in Mama's big green chair. It was my favorite chair, and I took plenty of good naps while the fan blew in my face in the summertime. I noticed Mr. Bill would look at me from time to time in the corner of his eye as he worked. I pretended I didn't see him checking out my legs with piercing eyes. I thought the elderly man was friendly, so I smiled back when I caught him peeking at me the fifth time.

"Yes, her mother passed away when she was only two years old. She was sick," Mama replied. "But she's mine, and she keeps me young."

"That's good. I pray God will bless you."

"He already has been blessing me, and He has never stopped," Mama said sweetly before her tone changed to serious. "Pray that God takes away that spirit of perversion you have."

Oooooh, Mama was so mean when she said it through her tight lips.

Mr. Bill's eyes bucked, and he was offended that he had been rebuked. He tried his best to prove that he was innocent.

"Ethel, I ain't a sick man. How could you accuse me of something like that?" he asked Mama.

"I didn't accuse you of anything. The Holy Spirit told me, if you don't straighten up, then you will surely burn in Hell," Mama said.

"Ethel, you don't have to worry about me coming in here to help you again," Bill said, slamming his toolbox shut.

"Good. Repent for the wages of sin is death!" Mama said. "I pray for your soul!"

It wasn't the first time Mama rebuked people and called out foul spirits. She once called out her pastor, and he didn't take it too kindly, but her correcting him saved his life. She also rebuked me and Leon for things we did.

Mama often said, "Your blood will not be on my hands."

Once Mr. Bill was gone for good, Mama took some blessing oil, rubbed it on the doorway, and began to pray loudly.

"Oh, precious Father God, in the name of Jesus-

Leon came out of his bedroom and pretended to have the Holy Ghost. I laughed on the inside about how he carried on and thrust his body back and forth, and then suddenly, he yelled, *"Thank You, Jesus!"* And by the way he jumped up and cried with his arms stretched out. I knew he wasn't faking anymore. Leon spoke in the Heavenly language. My brother was fire-baptized in our living room! Mama started clapping her hands and rejoicing with him!

"Did you catch the Holy Ghost, too?" Ivy asked.

"Not that time. I was too scared," Maple said.

The phone rang, so Maple went to answer it.

"Hey, there, Baby Sis," Leon sang happily.

"Hey, Leon. I was talking about you."

"If you're still talking about me catching the Holy Ghost in Mama's living room, you can let that go. That was years ago," he said, laughing. "Anyway, since I've been so busy, I'm trying to get there to see you. I miss you, Baby Sis."

"I miss you too, Leon."

EIGHT

"How are you feeling?" Honey asked.

"Taking it day by day," Ivy answered, folding her clothes and placing them on her bed. Thoughts ran rampant through her mind about how badly she wished for the worst to happen to Brian. The idea that he was living next door made her plot revenge. Sure, she knew she was wrong, but it felt so right to have his company at the time. He could laugh all he wanted to, but to have the last laugh bothered her.

"Are you worried about your job interview?" Honey asked.

"Kind of," Ivy said.

Time was ticking, and Ivy's mother was concerned about her. It would only be a matter of time before she had to tell her family what had happened. A month passed, and Ivy's family believed she was still engaged and well cared for by a man who adored her.

"Sometimes things don't work out how you believe they should because it works out better than you can imagine," Honey said, sitting beside her on the bed.

"Is that what your mother used to tell you?" Ivy asked.

Honey smiled, "Oh, you think you're slick. You want me to finish telling you about my life."

"Well, you can't start and not finish," Ivy said.

"Hmm, where should I pick up? Ah, yes, the night before Thanksgiving," Honey said.

"Dessie, you know you can make this pie just like Mama did," Gayle said.

"We won't have any left for tomorrow," Sweetie agreed, eating her a slice of peach pie.

Dessie chuckled while she prepared the morning's food. She laughed so much with her sister that her cheeks started to hurt.

"I want to thank y'all again for coming down to see me. The holidays wouldn't have been the same," Dessie said, sitting at the kitchen table. She had a bowl full of peas in front of her that she planned on cooking.

"We ain't had nothing else to do. I don't have a family and Sweetie doesn't either," Gayle said. "And you thanked us enough."

"And our nieces are growing up so fast. I missed them too," Sweetie said.

Gayle said, "Yes, and Clara looks like you and-

The room finally went silent.

"Erica looks a little like you too, Dessie," Sweetie said, trying to break the awkward moment.

"Where?" Gayle asked rudely. "Erica looks just like her daddy's folks. It ain't no denying it." Gayle slapped the table as if her point was made final.

"Well, it's not her fault," Sweetie said. "She's still a beautiful girl."

"Ain't nobody said anything about her being ugly. But, the truth is *the damn truth.*"

Dessie sat quietly and wanted the conversation to end, but Gayle kept running her big mouth. Sweetie looked at Gayle and tried to stop her from ranting, but it was useless. Gayle was in her mood of 'I said what I said, and you can kiss my ass if you don't like it.'

"Dessie, I can't see how you do it. I look at Erica and see what that man did to us—how he held us down and had his way!"

"Got dammit!" Dessie screamed and slammed her hand on the table, too. "I love Erica the same way I love Clara–and Clara's daddy held me down and raped me too. You think having two daughters by felons was easy to live with. You can *leave* if my daughter Erica bothers you so much."

"You're gonna put me out, huh? How are you going to threaten to put me out?" Gayle put her small, square glass of brown liquor on the table and wiped her mouth. "You don't do that to your sisters."

"My children come first," Dessie said without any hesitation.

"Are you sure about that? The first man who paid you any *real* attention, you packed your bags and left as soon as you could. You went from Motown to Coontown!"

"You don't understand. When I told Robert how my children were conceived, he still loved me. How many men do you know would take my hand in marriage? You can hide your scars in your heart, but my heart is open so the world can see my two gorgeous girls. You should have seen the looks on their faces when I told my daughters what happened."

"You told them?" Sweetie asked.

"Yes, because I wanted them to know the truth," Dessie said before weeping. "Ain't no sense of hiding it!"

"Dessie, I was wrong, and I'm so sorry," Gayle said, walking over to Dessie. "Please, forgive me."

"I wish I was old enough to know what happened. I swear to God I would have killed him. I wouldn't give a damn who he was. He ain't no uncle of ours, not by blood. But I sure would have loved to see his guts spilled all over the floor while I stapped the fuck out of him over and over again! Thank *God* he's in Hell now," Sweetie said, taking a swig of her drink.

They had never heard Sweetie talk violently with so much passion.

"I forgive you, Gayle. And I love you." Dessie said.

"Love you, too. I love my baby sisters with my whole heart," Gayle said.

They embraced each other and wiped tears.

Sweetie stomped her foot and clapped her hands. She smirked at her sisters and reminded them of a song they had made up when they were young girls in Detroit.

Sweetie began to sing;
"We the soul sisters, the...the soul sisters...
The soul sisters, yes, the soul sisters...
We Black, we Brown, we are beautiful—and can't nobody put us down... *because we are the soul sisters...soul...soul sisters."*

Mom and Gayle joined the singing, and they danced the night away.

That was when I learned to laugh through the pain, not heal it, but laugh and dance around it. My mama and Auntie Sweetie danced around the fire and ignored Aunt Gayle's burning grief. Instead of putting the fire out, they allowed it to brew and consume her. But they didn't know. None of us knew how to handle trauma.

Aunt Gayle wasn't able to bore children. Unfortunately, my sister, Erica, resembled the monster who touched them. But, Somehow, Aunt Gayle was expected to accept us, but we were *not* her children. Looking back at it, that wasn't fair to Aunt Gayle.

"Oh, my God," Ivy said, seeing Honey's head hanging down.

"No wonder why Aunt Gayle was mean sometimes. Could we blame her?" Honey asked. "For all of these years that passed, it finally made sense. Excuse me, Ivy." Honey left. She entered her bedroom to have a moment of silence for

Gayle. Oh, how she wished she could turn back the hands of time and love on her more.

Honey regretted that she promised Ivy that she would recant her life. It was far too heavy and gut-wrenching, and there was a much longer way to go. She didn't even get to the sad part or...the part where...*or*...the part where-

I can't do this, Honey thought.

Later that evening, Honey called Maple.

"What's wrong, girl?" Maple asked. She knew her friend was troubled to call so late in the evening.

"We helped a lot of girls, but Ivy is different. She's the only one who asked us about our lives. The only one who cared about where we came from," Honey said.

"That's true," Maple agreed.

"Maple, we thought we were helping Ivy. But what if Ivy was sent to help us?"

NINE

"It's kind of strange how you've been outside so much lately," Ivy said, talking to Brian across the fence. She saw Brian sitting on his porch, pretending to read a book. As long as Ivy lived there, Brian did no such thing. He loved Ivy's misery, and as long as she was at Honey's house, he was going to manipulate her mind.

Brian shook his head and said, "Come on, I have no reason to worry about you. This is my yard, and I can enjoy my lawn."

"I hope you enjoy the gates of hell."

"As long as you're not my neighbor there, too."

"Fuck you."

"You already did. Three to five times a day."

"I hope that bee stings you in your neck," Ivy said.

Brian flapped the book all around himself and was embarrassed when he learned that Ivy had lied about the bee.

Ivy laughed as she crossed the yard and knocked on Maple's door.

"Hilarious, Ivy!" Brian screamed before he entered his house.

"You're still entertaining that blockhead fool," Maple said, opening the door. "He must have put it on you real good."

"Yes, he did," Ivy whispered. "But I still hate his guts."

Maple laughed, "Girl, if you don't forgive yourself, let it go. You do know how to please yourself, don't you?"

"Ms. Maple!"

"What? I'm old, but I ain't dead yet. C'mon, could you try on this dress? My client is about your size. I swear you girls eat grapes and drink water all day."

"Not since I've been staying with Ms. Honey," Ivy said, grabbing the dress to try on. "By the way, how did y'all meet?"

"I can't tell you now because I'll ruin the rest of the story."

Ivy slipped on the red dress, "This is beautiful."

Maple examined her work. "Still not right. I need to hem it a little bit more on the sides. Okay, you can take it off."

"So, your mama really got you into fashion, huh?" Ivy asked.

"Yes, she did."

"Come here, Anna," Ethel said.

Mama took out the dress I had ruined and made it look new. I looked for the hole, but I didn't see it. I was amazed.

"How did you do this?" I asked.

"God gave me a gift. Maybe you won't be playing around in your nice clothes next time."

"Thank you, Mama." I hugged her and admired the dress like I never had it. From then on, I watched Mama sew pants, skirts, mittens, and blankets. She was creative.

Some nights, I'd sit on the side of her long feet while she stitched fabrics together. She weaved the needle and gently stitched each patch, showing me she was more patient than I thought.

Sometime later, when she thought I wasn't going to stick myself, I tried my hand at it.

"Okay, slow down, Anna. You want to get a rhythm going. There you go."

I was practicing on my old doll's clothes. I took the brown thread and began to learn my newly found passion.

"This is fun," I said, looking up only to get stuck by the needle. I screeched a little.

"It's okay, it's okay," Mama said, wrapping my finger around a rag. "You did an excellent job."

I looked at my finger and giggled. I wasn't going to allow one prick to stop me from being gifted like Mama. I'd prick my finger a million times before I quit.

"Let's call it a day. I have to go shopping for a hat."

Mama loved hats, and I loved shopping, too.

"Leon, are you coming with us?" Mama asked.

"No way...you both take too long," he said.

"Well, you know the rules. Your sister and I will be back soon."

"Soon? Yeah, right," he said.

"Hush your mouth," Mama said and laughed because she knew it was true.

Mama enjoyed an outing and eating ice cream with me.

Mama was so tall that I was at her hip when we strolled down the street. I couldn't help but notice the attention she was getting from others, too. She never slouched, and her chin was held high all the while she held my hand.

"Good evening, miss. How are you doing today?" An older gentleman asked.

I didn't have enough fingers and toes to count on to say how many times he spoke to Mama over the years. He was intrigued by Mama's presence and was flirty.

"I'm fine, sir. Thanks for asking," Mama said, smiling as she kept going.

We continued window shopping until something caught her eye.

"That's a sharp-looking hat, right there," Mama said as we entered the store.

I clenched Mama's hand tighter. The white saleswoman wasn't too kind to see our faces. I saw her in the corner of my eyes while she tooted her nose and never greeted us.

Mama adored the white hat and was about to pick it off the mannequin.

"Excuse me, *Negroes* are not allowed to touch anything without buying it," she said. "If you want to try it on, you must wear a scarf."

Mama knew the rules and tried on many hats, but she was always allowed to touch them.

Mama replied kindly, "I can tell by the way this hat sits that only a woman with a dark hue and a head full of thick hair can give this style any justice. How much is this hat?"

"It's twenty-five dollars," she said rudely, holding her hands on her hip.

I saw the price was ten.

Mama dug inside her purse and counted her money. "God blessed me with just enough. Too bad a colored woman's life is priceless. I'll happily excuse myself," Mama said.

We left the store, and before we got to the end of the street, I said, "I hate how that woman talked to you. I wish I could give her a knot on those thin, ugly lips!"

Mama quickly grabbed me and turned me around. She stooped down and fussed, "Hush, your mouth, girl. God can deal with anybody more than you can. Forgive them, for they do not know what they do. Do you hear me?"

"Yes, ma'am," I said reluctantly.

"Now, let's go get us some ice cream so you can cool your hot tail down."

Maple's story was interrupted by a thud at her front door.

"I wonder who this could be," Maple said. She peeked through the peephole. "Who's there?" Slowly, she opened the door and saw Jasmine, who had passed out lying on her back.

"Jasmine, Jasmine!"

Jasmine was rushed to the emergency room, and Maple was informed that her daughter had a high temperature and was severely dehydrated. While Jasmine lay down on the bed asleep, Maple sat by her side along with Honey.

"My God," Maple said, begging God to amend their relationship before it was too late.

Maple had so many questions. Where had she been? How did she get home? Who had she been with?

"It's going to be okay, Maple," Honey assured her. "She's still here for a reason."

Maple stroked Jasmine's thick, short hair and whispered in her ear, "Mama will always love you. Please forgive me. I was young and foolish."

TEN

"You look mighty fine for an interview. Aren't you a little too overdressed to become a waitress?" Brian teased, watching Ivy walk into Honey's yard.

"You know what, Brian, you should have kept a few skirts and a pair of heels because you're a bitch!" She fired back before entering the house. "Good evening, Ms. Honey," she said, smiling.

"How did your interview go?" Honey asked.

Ivy flung her shoes off and sat on the couch. "I think it went well. I do have some sales experience," she said.

Ivy's cell phone rang, but she ignored the call.

"Can't keep pushing it away," Honey said.

"I've been talking to her all day. My mom knows that I'm fine."

"But, she knows when something is wrong. Mothers get that feeling about their children," she said. Honey went into the kitchen and poured Ivy a glass of water. "We are going to believe God for that job."

"Amen," Ivy whispered. "I've been worried about Ms. Maple. I hope her daughter will be okay."

"I saw miracles happen. They come in so many different ways. Now, I can look back and see how God provided so many times," Honey said, shaking her head. "I'd never forget Christmas...

Since that horrible conversation, my mama and aunts have been in good, cheerful spirits, again. We opened gifts, ate, and sang Christmas carols throughout the house. My sister and I were having one of the best holiday seasons ever. We unwrapped many clothes and dolls while the grown folks danced around the tree and got drunk from spiked eggnog. It was mostly Mr. Morgan's family and friends there, but they were friendly and glad that Mr. Morgan found the woman of his dreams, my mama. I was floored when Mr.

Morgan gifted me a pink bike I had been asking for. Mama said I had to get good grades in school, but I knew that wouldn't happen, so I dreamed about the bike, not knowing it would come true one day.

"That's too much. Why would you give her something like that?" Dessie asked, complaining. Almost every gift she opened, she'd say, "You really didn't have to buy me this, or this was too sweet of you."

"Just shut up and say thank you," Gayle said, making everyone laugh.

As far as my Aunt Sweetie, she had her eye on Mr. Morgan's cousin. When everybody was inside, they snuck on the porch to converse.

"So, they call you Sweetie," Von said, talking kindly.

"Yes, they do. And, actually, Sweetie is my real name," she said.

I always overheard how Aunt Sweetie liked her men, and Von was the ideal guy. He was tall, not too thin or big, with a beard, well-dressed, and borderline ugly. Oh, and Sweetie wanted her man so damn dark he'd have to open his eyes at midnight to reveal himself.

"So, are you really sweet?" he asked, licking his lips. "I'm sorry. Not that I'm trying to be seductive, but my lips are kind of dry," he said.

"No offense at all. I just wonder what a 'bama nigga can do with a Motor City girl like me," she said, leaning on the rail and tooting her behind in the air.

"Well, I keep good and strong, if you know what I mean. I grew up on a farm where I was taught how to plow," he flirted, moving his coat out of the way and sticking out his pelvis. "Now, this is me being seductive."

They laughed.

"Seriously, you're the most beautiful woman I've ever seen. It would be my pleasure to take you out," Von said.

Sweetie hesitated for a while before she answered, "I guess so."

"Come on in the house, Sweetie. We got to give Dessie her last gift," Gayle Announced. "We have a lovely surprise for our sister. Everybody gather around, please," Gayle said.

Sweetie grabbed the small box and handed it to my mama, who was pleased and curious about the wrapped gift.

"Hurry up and open it," Sweetie said. "You get on my nerves because you always take your precious time to do everything."

"I love to savor the moment," Dessie teased. She unraveled the box and pulled out a pearl necklace.

"This is Mama's necklace," Dessie said. "Why are you two giving this to me?"

"Because you're the first to get married," Gayle said. "Stop acting like you don't remember the promise we made when we were little girls."

"Yes, the first to get married gets to have Mama's pearls," Sweetie said.

"So, you better hurry up!" Von teased.

"This is so nice," Dessie said. She tried not to cry, but the sweet gesture was too overwhelming. She wished her parents could see her walking down the aisle.

Gayle snapped it around Dessie's neck.

"Isn't she lovely?" Sweetie asked Mr. Morgan.

Mr. Morgan sat on the other end of the dining room table. He sat there sullen. I was still determining what was on his mind. We were all clueless.

"Open your damn mouth," Gayle demanded. "You got your man so speechless." Gayle nudged Mama on her shoulder to ease the sudden strange mood that settled in the house.

Mama waited for him to speak. We all waited for him to say something.

"I don't want to get married," Mr. Morgan whispered, gazing across the room above Mama's head.

"What did you say?" Sweetie asked, stepping closer to Mr. Morgan and lowering her head to hear him better.

"I don't want to get married," Mr. Morgan repeated, looking at Mama. "I'm sorry, Dessie, but you gotta find someone else."

"I know you fucking lying!" Gayle screamed. "My sister moved her entire life to marry your coon licking, neck-bone-sucking *ass*, and this is the way you do her!"

"What a damn disgrace?" Sweetie said. She got up from the table and rubbed Mama's back. "Dessie, I am so sorry."

My mama sat there stone-faced while she clutched her pearl.

"Cousin, may I ask why?" Von asked. "This ain't right. We don't do stuff like this. We pride ourselves on being gentlemen. All you ever did was talk about how you loved Dessie."

"I can't do it," Mr. Morgan said. "And I lost...I lost my will so that I could send enough prayers to God to give Dessie and her girls the protection that they needed. It would kill me if something were to happen and I couldn't defend them. I go to my job every day, and I can't look the white men in the eyes. How can I be the king of my household when I can't face the Devil? Every *damn* day at work, I respond to boy and nigger, and I can't say anything because I am no longer living just for me. And what if one day I snap and want to walk away and start all over? But I can't. I would have to swallow my pride because I would have a family to feed. And I don't need nobody nagging at me."

"I don't nag," Dessie said.

"You don't do it now, but one day you will. That's what all women do- they nag and whine. I saw it for myself. I saw it too many times for myself. So, let me be my own disappointment. Let me be the man in my own damn head!" Mr. Morgan yelled. He looked at Von and said, "Because we all know it's a lie. We ain't got no kind of place in this world. If I can't protect her, what's the point of being her husband?"

"Fine time to tell her," Sweetie snapped.

"Just sorry, just low-down and sorry as hell," Gayle fussed. "You black-

"Enough!" Dessie yelled.

Once Dessie had everyone's attention, she spoke lightly, "You heard the man. He doesn't want to marry me. He proved that my girls and I were not worth fighting for. And that's okay. That's absolutely fine. But I want you to know that I loved you and was willing to stand with you through the roughest moments of your life. I would stand strong and be the wife you needed in the most trying times. I swear I was. But *you* don't deserve me because you're a coward. My girls and I will be packed and ready to leave very soon," Dessie said, unsnapping the pearl from around her neck. She handed it to Sweetie and said, "Merry Christmas, everybody."

"So, that's how you ended back in Detroit?" Ivy asked.

"Yes," Honey said. "A week later, we left Mr. Morgan as if he was a stranger. But Aunt Sweetie stayed behind to be with Von a little longer."

"Sweetie really did fall in love, huh?" Ivy asked. "I love to listen to how love birds meet."

"Ivy...this ain't no damn love story," Honey said.

ELEVEN

When Jasmine was released from the hospital, Maple convinced her to come home and get fully well. Maple thought about the times she almost lost her daughter and the many nights she cried, wondering where she was. Although she wished to hug and love her even more, she gave Jasmine space. Maple didn't want to run her away so soon. Maple showed patience, checked on her every once in a while, and used gentle, simple words.

"Do you need anything?" Maple asked.

Jasmine sat sullenly in the bedroom and looked out the window into the backyard. She was strangely entertained by a baby black bird that flew freely back and forth from one end of the gate to the other. She thought about how the bird had once been kicked out of the nest and had to take flight. The bird survived and had the opportunity to travel the world, but it remained on that old, leaning gate.

Jasmine secretly cheered for the bird to soar higher, spread her wings, and find a sense of belonging somewhere else, far from there.

Jasmine thought about her life. She beat the opposition of being a foster kid but never took flight.

Suddenly, the bird launched into the air and chirped away.

"No, thank you," Jasmine said quietly. She never looked at her mother.

"Okay, let me know if you need anything," Maple said.

"They took her away from me," Jasmine whispered.

Maple turned around and asked, "Jasmine, did you say something?"

"They took her away from me," Jasmine said, turning her head towards her mother. "I held her, and I rocked her cold body until they had to snatch her away from me. They took her away from me because I didn't want to let her go," she cried as she held out her hands. "They took my precious, dead baby away from me. I begged and pleaded to give me a little while longer to...to...to say that I love my baby," she cried, holding her heart.

"Jasmine, I am so sorry," Maple said, watching her troubled daughter, who was now on her knees crying towards the ceiling.

Maple tried to comfort her.

"Get away from me!" Jasmine snapped. "My baby was dead and couldn't feel or hear me speak to her, and I didn't want to let her go. I wasn't ready to say goodbye. *I needed* my baby!"

Maple held her hand over her head and leaned against the wall. Her daughter experienced the worst pain that no one could imagine, and she wasn't there to be with her. In agony, she listened to Jasmine.

"But there I was, a child full of emotion, and you looked me straight in the eyes and let them take me! What kind of mother were you? You waited until I could feel what love was, and then you crushed my heart. I'd never forgive you," Jasmine said. She hurried off the floor and snatched her bag out of the closet.

"Jasmine, will you please allow me to explain-

"That you were a horrible mother. Is that all? I *hate* you!"

"Jasmine."

Jasmine carried her bag on her shoulders and left.

Ivy happened to see Jasmine rushing down the street to God knows where. She wondered how such a lovely woman could have such a daughter who despised her. Her heart went out to Maple, and she could not say any words to ease the pain. Then, Ivy thought about the Bible that Honey had given her.

Maybe the words are inside of it, Ivy thought.

The following day, Honey saw Ivy pacing the floor and checking her phone.

"You still haven't heard from the job," Honey said. "Don't let it bother you."

"I put in more applications just in case," Ivy said, sitting on the couch. "I folded the blankets already, I mopped the floor and washed the dishes. I did everything but get on my knees and scrubbed the base of the walls, which I'm about to do in a few," Ivy said.

Ivy cleaned the entire house to keep her mind occupied. Although Honey said she didn't mind her, she felt terrible for freeloading on her.

"So, Ms. Honey, what happened when you returned to Detroit?"

"Oh, I was waiting for you to ask me," Honey replied, sitting beside Ivy. She picked up her story where she left off.

Although Mama's relationship with Mr. Morgan didn't work out, I was happy to be out of the South. We got settled into Aunt Gayle's house.

Aunt Gayle had a lovely home, too. It nearly blew Mama's mind when she saw she was on the nicer side of town. When Mama used to ask about the house, Aunt Gayle would say, "Oh, just a little house to keep warm." So Mama assumed it was nothing to brag about. But the four-bedroom brick house was something I could have gotten used to.

"My girls and I will be out of your way soon," Dessie said. "I know there's some dusting and cleaning that I need to do at Mama's house. Did you hear me, Gayle?" Dessie asked.

Gayle didn't say anything. Instead, she turned her back and hung her head away from Mama.

"Gayle, every time you look like that, something is wrong. What do I not know?" Dessie asked, folding her arms.

It took Gayle a moment to answer.

"Sweetie and I sold the house," Gayle confessed.

At first, Dessie didn't say a word. "You and Sweetie did what? Turn around! You are bad enough to do it behind my back, then be bad enough to tell me like a woman," she said, dropping her purse on the floor.

"Sweetie and I sold the house, Dessie. I'm sorry-

"Some damn sisters yall are. How could you two go behind me and sell the house without me knowing? Where's my money?" Dessie asked, holding out her hand.

"It wasn't much."

"I don't care if it was a *damn* dime. Where is my money, Gayle?" Dessie still had her hand out. "When our parents were sick, *I* was there. *I* sacrificed my life and waited on Mama *hand* and *foot*-and you two didn't have the decency to tell me the house was sold!"

"Please, don't blame Sweetie. It was all my fault. I told her that I was giving you your part. But Dessie, I didn't think you needed it. You moved and had-

"You're right, *I had*! Now, I don't *have* anything, now," Dessie threw her hands in the air.

Gayle sucked up her tears. "You and your girls can stay here as long as you want."

"Well, thank you so much for your kindness," Dessie said sarcastically. "It's the least you can do for robbing me of my inheritance. What a mess you are? And Sweetie was a fool for trusting you. This is going to take everything in me to forgive you." Dessie stormed out of the living room.

Mama looked at me straight into my eyes, and I saw the disappointment coloring her face. She saw me, and I could tell she wished I wasn't there to see how distraught she was. After everything she had done, her sisters had betrayed her.

"Mama might be down, but Mama is going to win," she said and hurried out of the door in the cold air.

"Mama did forgive her, but still, to this day, I don't know if it was because she loved her or because she had no choice," Honey said.

Honey felt herself fainting.

"Ms. Honey!" Ivy shouted. "Are you okay?" She fanned Honey with her hand to cool her down.

"Yes, I'm fine."

Ivy went into the kitchen and poured Honey a glass of water. "Are you sure everything is okay?" Ivy asked.

"Yes. It seemed like I could feel Mama's hurt all over again," Honey said.

Honey saw her mama's face painted perfectly in her memory, as if it were yesterday when she gazed into her little eyes and told her, "Mama is going to win."

That was all Honey wanted to see.

"Ms. Honey, you don't have to tell me anything else. I promise I'm good," Ivy said, thinking it was too overwhelming for Honey to continue.

"Ivy, there is no turning back. I carried this story inside of me for the longest time. I must go on."

TWELVE

One evening, Ivy went to Maple's house to help her sort some fabrics. Maple had been working a lot lately to keep her mind busy.

"This one is my favorite," Ivy said, rubbing Tally's dress in the corner. Maple looked over and imagined Tally wearing it and Tally's wide smile when she tried it on.

"Well, hopefully, she'll be here to pick it up," Maple whispered. She sighed a little, and her worry grew a tad more. She hadn't seen or heard from Tally since she refused to hand her the dress. She hoped she had no dealings with that man. It would be such a shame for her not to know that she deserved better.

After a short moment, Maple decided to take a break.

It seemed like Ivy wasn't leaving anytime soon, so they sat on the back porch and chatted for a while, then Maple began telling her story...

Mama and I would go to the market together every other Saturday. We stopped at Perez Market to get some fresh, sweet fruit.

"Hey, Mrs. Washington, what can I get for you today," Josea asked.

Josea was Hispanic, with a head full of black hair and charming dimples matted on his face. He was the owner's son, and I had seen him many times, but I saw him in a much different light that day. It was the first time I had been mesmerized by someone's appearance. I imagined it was the way Leon felt about Clarissa. My eyes were fixated on him. I watched every move he made, picking up produce and placing it into brown bags.

"We got a nice big watermelon. I thumped it, and it was hollow," Josea said, indicating that the fruit was ripe. He knew Mama was coming, so he hid the best-looking food in the back until she came.

Mama had favor with almost everyone. "You do right by God, and He'll make people do right by you," Mama told me, including enemies.

"No, thank you. I don't want to fool with a watermelon. Please give me some green grapes, oranges, and bananas," Mama said.

The green grapes were for Leon and me. We'd go to the backyard and toss the fruit into each other's mouths.

"No problem, I'll throw you in a couple of pecans, too," Josea said.

I watched him load the fruit into the brown paper bags. I wondered if his lips were sweet like those strawberries before me. I held my head down and felt ashamed of what I imagined. I could hear Mama scorning me for the sinful actions I had in my head.

"You're too kind," Mama said, taking the bags and paying him. She handed me one of the bags to hold.

"No problem," Josea replied. He waved at me, and my palms were sweaty as I blushed.

"Tell your daddy I said hey," Mama said.

"I sure will."

After we finished at the market, we headed to get ice cream. I ordered the chocolate fudge, and Mama had vanilla with caramel. I was strangely quiet outside, sitting by the window. I wondered if Josea thought I was cute. I turned to the right and saw my reflection in the shop's window. I had to make sure Mama wasn't telling me small fibs about how pretty I was. I studied hard on my face, my hair, and my weight.

I was only thirteen years old. Josea was an older teenager, maybe sixteen, no older than eighteen at the time. I had my first crush.

"He was a handsome young man, wasn't he?" Mama asked as if she had read my thoughts.

I was too shy and embarrassed to answer. How did Mama know that I thought Josea was cute? What did I do to give it away? Is she going to rebuke me?

"Come on, I'm not that old. I saw the way you looked at him. What? You don't think I'm so Holy that I would forget that one day you're going to start liking boys, do you?" she asked. She assured me that it was okay to have those feelings.

"He was kind of cute," I said softly, turning my head down to look at my half-empty bowl of ice cream.

Mama laughed at my actions, so I giggled loudly.

"You're growing into a young woman, and that's okay. I just want you to find a gentleman who will treat you with the utmost respect when it's time for you to date," Mama said, dipping her spoon into her ice cream.

"Is that why you're not dating?" I asked. I thought about all those men who would whistle at Mama and slide their way over to get her attention.

"Your grandpa gave me enough love to last me a lifetime," she said. "I miss him so much."

Before I could say anything else, she started talking about him. I listened. Tuskegee, Alabama - 1947

"Baby! Baby! Look at me," John said, admiring himself in the mirror.

"I'm a fine ass man, ain't I?" He wore a pinstripe black suit and admired his

chocolate flesh. His slight smile showed the tiny gap between his teeth.

"I'd say that I'm the luckiest woman in the world. So, glad to have you from that war," Ethel said, combing her shoulder-length hair. "Now that the kids are with my sister, I'd love to have you drop your bombs inside of me tonight," she said, grabbing his crotch.

"You keep talking like that and looking like you do. We might not make it out tonight," he flirted, then kissed her.

"It's been a long time since we had fun outside of the bedroom. So, let's go out and behave ourselves." She smiled and placed his hat on his head.

John and Ethel loved to dance, and they were the most loving Black couple in Tuskegee, Alabama. They'd hit the dance floor at a shaggy wooden club, and everybody would stop and watch the way they intertwined.

Ethel spread her wide hips and scooted down on her husband's lap as they rocked the night to the blues.

"I hope my wife doesn't find out that I'm dancin' with a fine ass woman," John whispered in her ear, playing a stranger.

"I don't give a damn about your wife," Ethel said, "I want you to come to my house tonight and use me like a slut. I want you to know what fuckin' a real woman feels like," she said, licking her tongue on his face.

"Oh, shit. I better go and get me something to drink," John said. He slapped her on the butt, and they went their separate ways.

Ethel rested her feet and didn't realize she sat next to Rita, who had a thing for sleeping around. Rita locked eyes with men and lured them between her legs like slapping together a peanut butter and jelly sandwich.

"Oh, chile, the way your husband dances, I know he can fuck good," Rita said. She was half-drunk but a total whore.

"Excuse me," Ethel said. "That's none of your damn business. And I'd advise you to take that thought out of your head. What my man can do ain't got shit to do with you. Do you understand me?"

"So, uptight. We are all just having a good time," Rita said, knowing she wanted John.

"Well, there's a line that you shouldn't cross." Ethel got up and went to the bar and ordered a drink to keep from choking Rita's neck.

"Don't let her get to you. If any man ain't faithful around here, John is," Diane said, placing the drink on the counter. "She's a homewrecker or looking to be a third party if you know what I mean."

"Her nasty ass tried the wrong one." Ethel drank her whiskey and took out her cigarette.

Diane lit it for her.

"Well, well, look who is coming in," Diane said, pointing at Oscar. "Haven't seen you in a mighty long time."

Oscar was sharply dressed in his gray suit. He sat next to Ethel at the wide bar table and greeted her with a side hug.

"Give me a beer, Diane," he ordered. "Nice to see you, Ethel."

"Same here," Ethel said, puffing her cigarette. "I'm so sorry to hear about your wife's passing."

"Yeah, I am, too. More than the war, I'm scared of dying alone. I pray that I keep my mind. Lord, help me to keep my mind," Oscar said, twirling his drink around. He had to force himself to leave the house and start living.

Ethel laid her hand on top of his hand and said, "Oscar, you've been like a brother to my husband. There's no way in hell I'll let you be alone. You're a great man, and you're handsome too. I'm sure you'll find someone who will love you soon."

"Thank you, Ethel. That is a mighty kind thing of you to say," Oscar said.

When Ethel and John got home that night, John was drunk and talking crazy. "Have you ever thought about spicing it up a little?"

"John, we have four kids. What are you talking about?"

"Well, I was talking to the fellas and they said, you know, women sometimes like to satisfy their man and bring, you know...you know, another woman into the equation."

"John, you're drunk, and you're talking stupid. It doesn't make any sense to survive a war and then get killed by your wife. I suppose you go to bed before you go to hell. Now, good night, sir."

Ethel swept the kitchen floor the following day and listened to John apologizing.

"I ain't worried about that. I knew it was the liquor talking," Ethel said.

John insisted that it wasn't an excuse.

"I'm sure hungry," John said, rubbing his stomach. He wondered why he didn't smell anything cooking. They had a few hours of alone time before his sister-in-law brought the kids home.

"You should go find that other woman to cook," Ethel said, slapping him lightly on his face.

"That's a good one. Let's stop drinking. It ain't good for a man to come back from the war and start all that drinking, you know."

"Speak for yourself. I ain't been to war unless you want to count screaming children running around this house."

"C'mon now, Ethel. We did everything together. Well, not everything, but you get me, right?"

Ethel wasn't willing to get rid of her drinking habit. She bragged that she could handle her liquor and still be helpful to her husband and children.

"What made you come up with this all of a sudden?" Ethel asked.

"Well, I told the good Lord if I made it back safely, I would give my life to Him. It doesn't mean we can stop having fun, but I got to meet the Lord halfway on something. I made a deal with Him and can't turn back."

Ethel glanced at her husband and saw that he was serious. She told him yes and that she'd try her best to stop drinking, but she wasn't making any promises.

"Your grandpa sounded like a wonderful man," Ivy said.

"Yes, he was. I imagined. Of course, Mama wasn't going to tell me everything, but as I got older, I learned to read between the lines, if you know what I mean," Maple said.

Ivy's cell phone rang. She saw it was for the job she had interviewed for, so she got up and answered it.

"Hello...this is her," Ivy answered, clenching her eyes. "Okay, thank you," she said, hanging up the phone.

"Well," Maple said.

"I got the job!"

THIRTEEN

Ivy tried on clothes to get ready for her work week. She feared she had gained too much weight from eating Honey's food. But, to her surprise, after one giant leap, the button on her pants snapped around her waist.

She was thrilled that she would be independent enough to help Ms. Honey and find her own little place. Anything was better than going back home.

She placed her blue blazer on and asked Honey, "How do I look?"

"Like a schoolgirl," Honey said. "Somewhat, like my sister Erica. Erica was smart, and I struggled all through school. That learning shit wasn't for me."

Honey smiled and continued her story.

Aunt Gayle moved us into another school district, making education more challenging. I always resented going to my classes, but Erica was a scholar. She made straight A's and was a great artist, too. She could draw about anything that I imagined. As for me, I would post a B plus on the refrigerator and wonder how in the hell did I make that score.

Mama never made me feel horrible about being academically challenged, and Erica, a willing teacher, offered to tutor me. I was already a grade behind, so I allowed her to help me, but she really worked my last nerves the way she carried on and ranted about the importance of having a good education.

She was so poised, and I was the opposite.

"Today, we are working on reading," Erica said, placing the books and dictionary before me. By the grace of God, I made it to the fourth grade.

I overheard my teacher say that I was reading at the second-grade level. I ran home, cried, and told my family that I was stupid and that I would never return to school.

"You're not stupid. You have to learn differently," Erica said, lifting my head up. "I'll teach you."

She kept her promise.

On Wednesday nights, we practice reading. She sat next to me in our bedroom, creating a desk in the corner. On the desk, she engraved affirmations on top of the wooden table. I am smart, I have good grades, and I am successful. I read this every day and wish it was true.

One night, I attempted to read and did so awfully that I wanted to cry, toss the book into the trash can, and burn it.

Erica always had patience.

"Sound it out, sister," Erica said nicely.

I attempted to sound out the word. "Ahhh-aq-qu-

She grabbed a pen and told me to write the word, so I did.

"Quarrel," Erica said, "the word is quarrel."

She picked up the paper and read my handwriting.

I sat back, pouted my lips, and folded my arms.

Erica was a great teacher and, most importantly, a wonderful sister. She believed in me and treated me better than I deserved. Occasionally, I would hide her homework or crumble up her artwork during chores. I hated that she was the smart one.

I could tell by how she looked at me and then spotted the word on the paper that something was wrong.

"Don't worry. That word might have been too difficult. I'm determined that you'll be great. Let's go over your spelling words," she suggested.

"I am tired," I said, pushing the book away. Sitting on the bed, I knew I was going to fail my spelling test on Friday. "Just leave me alone, please," I said rudely.

"L-O-V-E," Erica spelled the word.

"That spells love," I answered, "Everybody knows that one." I rolled my eyes and whispered, "I'm not *that* dumb."

"But does everybody know what it really means?" Erica asked. "You can know everything and not have a clue about things that really matter. This doesn't define you, Clara," she said, pointing at the dictionary. "Only you can shape your future. I love you so much that I don't care how mad you get. I'm still going to stick close by because I believe in you."

"Believe," I said. "That's one of my spelling words."

"What does that mean?"

I gave her my best answer, saying it was someone's feeling that something was possible.

She asked me, "What are you feeling?"

"Like an idiot," I said, looking at the words on the desk that told me lies. Those words made me more upset.

"Then you won't pass your test. But, what if I bet you that if you spell the word correctly, I'd make your bed for a week and wash the dishes, too.

"You promise," I said.

"I only said that because I know you won't spell it correctly," Erica said.

She knew I loved a challenge and hated washing the dishes.

I checked my inner feelings and trusted my brain that I could do it with all of my might. "Believe," I said. "B-E-L-I no, E. B-E-L-no, that's not right," I said, wrestling my thoughts. I shut my eyes to ignore my sister, smirking in the corner. "B-E-L-I-E-V-E!"

When I opened my eyes, I saw my sister cheering for me. She grabbed me and gave me a hug as if I had won the national spelling bee.

"That's all you have to do is believe, sister," Erica said.

But I had a long way to go.

"What's making you two so happy in there?" Aunt Gayle said.

It was nearly 10:30 that night, and her face was full of makeup. She looked gorgeous, and I barely recognized her wearing a knee-high black skirt.

Aunt Gayle never gave us a chance to answer before she ranted, "Auntie gotta work tonight. I'll see you two tomorrow. Y'all both be safe, do you hear me? Don't give your mama any trouble." Then, she left and hollered, "See you later, Dessie!"

"You two can go ahead and get ready for bed," Mama said.

Mama didn't want us to see how Aunt Gayle pranced out the door. But that was the first of many times Aunt Gayle left out half-dressed. Aunt Gayle didn't know it, but I slept lightly, and often, I'd see her staggering inside the house in the wee hours of the morning. Aunt Gayle crept inside a few times, telling men to hush up before they woke us.

One evening, Mama was getting dressed in her light blue work uniform. She found a job cleaning and cooking for an elderly lady at a house about three miles from Aunt Gayle's home.

Mama met Aunt Gayle inside of her bedroom, where Aunt Gayle started applying her makeup and humming the blues. She was getting ready for another night out.

"I have to work a little later today," Dessie said, pulling her belt tighter around her waist. "The girls will be alone for only a few hours."

Gayle paused and scanned her sister up and down as if her sister smelled awful.

"You should have left that country slave shit in the South," Gayle said, "Serving them white people. I could never do it."

"Well, to my surprise and yours, they are Black folks. Mrs. Margarete Johnston. I call her Ms. Sugar," Dessie said, smiling. "The sweetest old lady I ever met, and most of the time, we sit and chat. She wants somebody to listen to her. Besides, I'll do *almost* anything to feed my children."

Gayle stopped powdering her face, "You and your slick comments. So, what do you mean by that?"

"How long are you going to keep this up? You act like I have no idea what you're doing, and pretty soon the girls will find out."

"Dessie-

"Don't Dessie, me. We were not raised like that. Drinking and sexing-

"*I* now have the power in my hands and control what *I* do with my body. Men always look at me with desperate eyes, and there ain't no way in hell they will get it for free, never again! I got bills to pay and a roof to keep over my head. And if you hadn't noticed, we are some fine women, but we ain't smart worth a damn."

"Gayle, I am concerned about you." Dessie sat down in the long chair with her sister and wrapped her arms around her. "I don't want anybody to harm you. I need my sisters, and I'll do anything for you. Lord knows I have no room to judge, but why are you doing this?"

Gayle dropped her lipstick and sighed.

"When we were little girls, all we ever talked about was becoming mothers," Gayle said, looking down at her stomach. She slowly rubbed her left hand across her belly. "We talked about how we were going to raise our kids together, but that dirty motherfucker took that away from me," she cried. "He took it away from me, Dessie. My life will never be complete."

Dessie wrapped her arms tightly around her waist and wished she could do more to comfort her. She took a tissue and dampened Gayle's face.

"Aren't I still a woman?" Gayle asked, sobering. "I'm still a woman, aren't I, Dessie?... Am I *still* a got-damn woman?" she asked, sobbing and shaking.

"Yes, you are," Dessie replied softly. "The prettiest, bravest woman that I ever laid eyes on. You'll always be my rock," she said, squeezing Gayle's hand. "I love you so much and wish I could turn back the hands of time. You were hurt trying to save me. I owe you, Gayle. I owe you my life. And no matter what you do, I am going to love you. Sorry if I came off judgmental."

"We're both a crying mess," Gayle said, seeing her makeup smeared all over her face, drooping down on her red top.

"As long as we don't lay in it," Dessie said. "We can't lay in our mess, sister."

Sweetie called the house the following day, and joy rang throughout the home.

"Sweetie! I got Sweetie on the phone," Gayle called out.

Dessie approached the living room to hear her and asked, "When are you coming home, girl?"

"I'll be home next week. Von doesn't want me to travel alone," Sweetie said. "He is such a gentleman."

I heard her loud, pitched voice from the kitchen table, and I knew she was happy with that man.

"Seems like you two are taking it seriously," Gayle said.

"Well, I have some news. Promise that you two won't get mad," Sweetie said.

Dessie eased closer to the phone, "Go ahead, Sweetie. We both can hear you."

"I'm getting married!" Sweetie announced.

"Married?" Gayle said. "Why in the hell would you get engaged so damn soon?"

"Don't fuss at her, Gayle," Dessie said. She grabbed the phone. "Sweetie, I'm so happy for you."

"Happy! Who gets engaged after two months? A fool does! You don't know him," Gayle said, "hand me over the phone right now!"

Dessie gave the phone to her and sat on the sofa.

"It's her life," Dessie whispered.

"So, I guess you're moving there and not coming back," Gayle said, patting her foot.

"No," Sweetie said sternly. "He is moving to Detroit with me. I planned on a wedding shortly, but we didn't want to wait any longer, so he proposed. I can't explain it, but I am in love."

"Are you pregnant?" Gayle asked.

"So what if she is," Dessie said.

"I am not pregnant," Sweetie said. "I wanted to make my own decision, whether it was good or not. I stand by my choice to marry Von, and he is a damn good man, and if he isn't, then I'll keep moving until my husband finds me. Anyway, I was also calling to say that I miss my sisters and can't wait to return home."

"Well, congratulations, sister. I apologize, but as your sisters, I thought-

"No. Both of you thought for me long enough. Mama is gone, and I need to become my own woman," Sweetie said.

"I respect that, Sweetie, but as your older sister. I'm going to boss your ass one more time. Bring your high-yellow ass back home soon!"

They laughed for a good while. Dessie sat in the chair and shook her head.

"I love you, Sweetie," Gayle said.

"Love you!" Dessie hollered.

"Love y'all too!" Sweetie yelled.

Dessie and Gayle waited for their sister and Von to arrive. Dessie kept checking her watch and thought they would have been home. She hoped Sweetie's smart-talking ways did not get them into any trouble.

As usual, I kept looking outside and hoped I'd see her pull up in the driveway at any time in Von's car.

"Dessie, I have something for you," Gayle said, sitting close to her on the couch and handing her an envelope. "Go ahead and open it," Gayle said.

I saw from the corner of my eyes that it was a check.

"Uncle Richard sold some family property in Georgia, and that's all on Daddy's part. Since I didn't do right with the house, I decided to let you have it all. It is only fair," Gayle said.

"Thank you, Gayle. This is enough to get my children a little place of our own. It's a nice start."

"I don't always do things right, but if I can make it up, I will."

"You got that right."

The phone rang.

"This must be Sweetie," Gayle said. She answered the phone, and Von was on the other line.

"Gayle- *I...I...I* don't know how to tell you. Is Dessie around?"

"Yes, she's around," Gayle said, nervously waving for Mama to come closer. "What's going on? Von, is everything okay?"

I looked out the window and saw Aunt Sweetie in the driveway, wearing her fuzzy hat and pink dress suit. She was waving joyfully and smiling. In slow motion, she blew me a kiss and started fading into the background. That's when I realized it was her spirit saying goodbye. My tears slid down my brown, numbed face. I rushed outside, hoping to catch her before she was no more. I was too slow..

"There was a car accident. The man hit us and- Sweetie ain't make it. She is gone," Von sobbed.

The scream that I heard from Mama and Aunt Gayle, I'd never forget. It pierced my heart and stunned my ears," Honey said, weeping.

"My... dear... Aunt Sweetie...

"Oh, Ms. Honey," Ivy said, weeping with her.

At midnight, Honey had a dream.

"Hey, Clara," Sweetie sang, coming into Honey's bedroom. Her sweet fragrance lit the room, and her bright appearance gilded inside, along with her peaceful presence.

"Aunt Sweetie!" Honey sang out. Her 65-year-old self turned into that little girl who admired her auntie near and far.

"It's about time you mentioned my name," Sweetie said. " You acted like I was some kind of ghost," she joked. "Look at you, looking like your mama." She rubbed Honey's face. "I've been watching you and am proud of the woman you became."

"I miss you so much," Honey said, fixing her eyes on her. "I loved you so dearly. And I know I made a lot of mistakes."

"Be quiet, girl. Who knows what mistakes I would have made if I lived a little longer. I wanted to marry that man after two months." She laughed. "Seriously, you carried everything so well, and how you helped others amazes me. Don't you dare feel sorry for me? I lived my life, and nothing bothers me more than people sobering around like their time ain't coming too. Clara, I love you enough to let you know that you got more to live for, and I ain't trying to see you come on this side of life yet. I know you had days where you wanted to give up, but no, ma'am. You gotta keep going. Let me live through you for a while longer."

FOURTEEN

"You have a big day coming tomorrow," Maple said, cracking the window open to let a light breeze flow throughout the house.

"Tell me about it. I'm glad I can help out a little," Ivy said. She was anxious about her first day of work.

Ivy's obsession with Brain slowly faded, but a small part of her still desired him to be with her at night.

"It's nice having you around, Ivy. You turned out not to be so bad," Maple said and giggled. She thought about the first time they met. "You haven't given up on love, have you?" Maple asked.

"I don't think so," Ivy replied.

"Well, you will have ups and downs in all relationships. But if it's true love, then it will overpower the bad. My mama taught me that," Maple said, continuing the story of her mama and Grandpa John...

One evening, John pranced into the house. He danced to the kitchen, where he saw Ethel sweeping the floor. She was pregnant with their fifth child, who became Maples' mother.

"What has gotten into you?" Ethel asked.

John pulled out a paper out of his back pocket. "The Tuskegee Experiment," he said, then read, "Bad Blood. Negroes come and be a part of this experiment, and you will gain free rides to the doctor, food, and burial insurance. Ethel, this can be a ticket to help us out. In case something happens to me, it would be good to know that my family is covered and well-taken care of," he said proudly.

Ethel was not amused.

"Give me that," she told him. She read the paper and laid it on the table.

"What's the matter?" John asked.

"You mean to tell me that white people who treat us less than dogs all of a sudden care about us? I'm not too sure if I can trust this. Just last week, Randall was hit in the head with a wooden stick just for accidentally bumping into one of them. Now they want to treat us for bad blood and treat us for free?"

"Everything isn't about race. Maybe for once, being Black is a good thing," John argued. "I don't want to miss this opportunity to provide for my family."

"I'm not against it yet. Let us pray about it first." Ethel suggested.

"There you go, you want to pray about everything. Sometimes, it's just common sense, Ethel," John said. "Now, all I have to do is go down there in the morning and let them draw blood from me. It's just that simple, and if it's bad blood, I get treated. That's it."

"And that's the problem, when has it ever been easy for us and when have they ever been so nice? But, if you want to do it, then go right ahead-

"You never trust me to make any decisions around here anymore. You're always asking God. You bother Him more than you bother me."

"I told you, if you want to do it, then go right ahead-

"But you're saying it as if I'm making a bad decision. Ethel, you and my kids mean the world to me, and there's nothing I wouldn't do to provide."

"God has been helping you provide for us all of these years. We have never gone a day without a meal or out in the cold. So, if you feel like you want to do it, then go right ahead."

Later in the evening, John played checkers with Oscar on the porch. They were joined by Bob, a big guy who was a friend and a sharecropper. Bob sat on the bottom steps, chimed in on their conversation, and interrupted their game with his loud, infectious laughter.

"Well, I got bad blood," Bob said, "and they are treating me for it too. I get a free ride to the clinic, health care, and a hot meal."

"My wife ain't too sure if I should go down there," John said. "King me!"

"I don't blame her," Oscar said. "If I'm sick, and a shot of whiskey or gin can't heal me, then let me die." He took his black checker, jumped John's red checkers, and collected his pieces.

"Well, we have wives to take care of. That's the difference between us and you!" Bob fussed. "A poor Black man has to take advantage of every opportunity we can get."

"Well, the difference between us and you is that we ain't poor. We ain't rich either, but we ain't stupid, nigger poor," Oscar said.

John leaned back in his seat.

"Now, why would you say some bullshit like that to me, Oscar? As another nigger, why would you put me down? You're wrong for that. Oscar, your ass is just plain wrong! Cause I ain't got no shame in doing what the hell I got to do. I think you owe me an apology," Bob said.

"I apologize. I took my joke too far," Oscar said. "But you know damn well I miss my wife."

Oscar wasn't paying attention to the game, so John's red piece jumped his last black piece, and John won the game.

"Well, ain't that some shit," Oscar said. "Just like life, if a Black man doesn't pay attention, he's gonna be jumped over every time."

"What are yall out here fussing about?" Ethel asked, stepping out of the screen door.

"We are talking about the Tuskegee Experiment," John said. "Bob is doing it, and they are treating him well."

"I feel fine," Bob bragged.

"Tuh, bad blood? Was our blood bad when they tied us to trees and whipped us? My grandpa had lashes on his back that looked like a road of raw flesh. I'll never forget the day he showed me. It scarred me for life. Ain't no way, ain't no way in the hell I'll let a white man touch me for his gain," Oscar said.

Ethel prayed that John would forget about that experiment and move on with his life, and that's what happened. John never mentioned it again and saw that his wife was right. He saw his friends and neighbors die off one by one, and it was an awful time throughout the years. Black men were tricked, not treated.

Some years later, Bob died too. They gave Bob's wife fifty-four dollars for his burial, nothing else.

"In between that time, my mother, her name was Faye, was born with complications. According to the doctors, she wasn't supposed to live that long, but she made it to twenty-five years old. God kept her long enough to give birth to Leon and me," Maple said. "She passed away when I was only two years old. That's why Mama Ethel raised me."

FIFTEEN

"Good morning, everyone. This is our new sales associate, Ivy," Mylissa introduced her to the employees.

It was Ivy's first day at work. She waved to her new co-workers and told them she was glad to join the team. The first two introduced themselves quickly. One was named Lisa, and the other was named Joan. They continued hanging the clothes on the racket and made it no big deal that they had a new co-worker.

Their manager, Mylissa, gently guided her over to meet the other worker. "This is Tally, the assistant manager, and she will show you around," she said, and then she left them alone.

"Nice to meet you," Tally said. "I'm the one who's always doing her job." Tally wasn't too quiet about her statement.

"Nice to meet you, too."

Ivy looked around the boutique and wondered if the ladies would treat her nicely. It had been a while since she had been around women, and she knew how catty they could be in the workplace. She remembered Honey's advice, telling her, ' Co-workers are not your friends. Do your job and go home.' But there was something about Tally because she was enthused and energetic.

"There's nothing much to do. Have a random conversation, and someone is bound to leave with something," Tally said after showing her around the store. "My commission is always great," she bragged. "Have you ever worked in sales before?"

"A long time ago. It was children's clothes."

"Do you have any children?"

"No, I don't, and I'm single," Ivy answered, assuming the next question would be about her love life.

"What about you?" Ivy asked.

"I have no kids, and my love life is complicated. I'm still trying to make things work with this guy."

A car honked, interrupting their conversation. As Tally looked out the window, she saw that it was Russell.

"Oh, that's Russell, my complicated boyfriend," Tally said. "You can take your break, and I'll see you in an hour." Then she rushed out of the door and walked to the car.

Tally's personality changed quickly. Ivy assumed that something was rather odd with her behavior. She went from bubbly to anxious, as if she had to leave immediately.

Ivy found a local sandwich shop and sat in the corner. She realized that she never enjoyed her own company. Sitting alone with her thoughts in public was strange yet terrifying. She fought the urge to quit her job and moved back home. She wondered if she would have found comfort in facing the music and confessing her wrongdoing to her family.

When she settled down to enjoy her meal, she heard her name.

"Ivy."

It was Brian, and it took her all her might not to dash her iced tea in his face. She couldn't catch a break from that man, who suddenly ended up in a place where no one hardly ever goes.

"So, I guess you're trying to avoid the crowds too, huh?" he asked, laughing. "Sitting there, all alone and looking like you lost all your friends. So sad, huh? How's your little job going?"

"What's sad is that you are following me. Brian, I am done with you, and I don't think your so-called wife is coming back. You don't deserve love because you don't know what it is."

"Love is bringing my wife home where she should be," he said. "Which is why I am surprised that your family hasn't come searching for you yet. Nobody loves you, Ivy. Not one single, got-damn person on this earth."

Ivy's freedom blinked before her eyes when she grabbed the knife off the table and-

"Shit! Somebody, come and help," a woman screamed. Her elderly dad was choking at a table nearby. His daughter tried to beat him on his back, but it wasn't working.

The man's face was turning purple.

"I got him," Brian said, wrapping his arms under the man's chest. He did the heimlich maneuver several times before the chunks of food flew out his mouth.

The man caught his breath as his daughter thanked him for his help.

Just when I was about to kill the bastard, Ivy thought.

After the dramatic scene, Ivy clocked back into work and waited on Tally, until she got word that Tally took off for the rest of the day. So, she sat around and twirled her thumbs and envisioned that knife deep into Brian's neck. It was a close call.

When Ivy got to Honey's house, she dared not tell Honey about the incident. She got chills when she realized she was dangerously close to risking it all. And why? Brian wasn't worth it, but he made her sick to her stomach. She took a hot shower and prayed that God would keep her sanity.

The third work day arrived, and Tally was still a no show. Her co-workers said that she called out sick, but Ivy had a funny feeling that it wasn't the case. There was more to the story and she had hoped to see her again because Tally was the only one who showed interest in training her.

For the next day, she has only unstocked and folded clothes and been ignored. That routine continued for the rest of the week, and Ivy had no interest in coming back.

Ivy's week was long, and she was glad it was Friday evening. She sat on the couch and realized she hated working, but she had a point to prove that she could make it alone.

She grabbed a glass of red wine and conversed with Honey.

"I am so proud of you," Honey said. "Perseverance goes a long way."

"I hope so."

"Seems like something is on your mind," Honey said, sipping her wine. She missed her talks with her. Ivy kept her company, but she had no energy to stay awake.

"I miss you telling me about your story," Ivy said, smiling and getting comfortable. She reminded Honey where her story had left off, and Honey continued.

A couple of weeks passed by after we laid Aunt Sweetie to rest, and we sat sullen and barely spoke to each other. Nobody was willing to face a bright light being deemed too early. That's how I found out that life didn't give a damn about who you loved. If it was their time, then there's nothing you can do.

Almost every day, I cried that spring and failed the fourth grade.

Aunt Gayle started drinking more heavily and would leave for days and not return until random times. Her actions bothered Mama, who, in her words, 'had to get up and live for her daughters.' She could no longer tolerate her sister's self-destructive behaviors, so they argued again.

"So, you're going to leave me?" Gayle asked. "Can you stay a little while longer," she pleaded.

"I can't. Gayle, I gotta go. You started bringing strange men in here, and I have girls to look after," Dessie said. "Unless you're willing to stop, then I must leave."

It was true. Mama got home late from work, and a guy was asleep on the couch with his bare chest out and pants unzipped, showing his dirty boxers.

One night, I thought it was safe to leave my bedroom, so I went to the kitchen to grab something to drink. Out of nowhere, a man scared me half to death, holding my thirteen-year-old hips and touching my developing breasts. I snatched away from him, ran into the bedroom, and locked the door. Erica awakened, and I snuggled in her bed right next to her. We had no idea where Aunt Gayle was at the time or why she left us with a total stranger.

We were only safe if Mama was around.

"Dessie, these men know better than to touch my nieces," Gayle said. "They ain't that crazy."

"It's either me or them!"

"Dessie, we have nice, curvy hips and thick legs, but we ain't born with silver spoons or have the education to make it. There's nothing smart about us Brown's sisters. I gotta make it in this world the best damn way I know how."

"You sound like a fool."

"If being a fool is doing what I need to do to make a living, then I'll be that. I'm a proud whore, and ain't shit going to stop me from living my life. Do you hear me? You came back with nothing. How in the hell did you think you got on your feet? Mr. Morgan and I provided for your children, not you! And if you think you can make it in this world, wiping houses down from top to bottom, then go right ahead. I would rather be whore any day than a slave monkey."

Dessie slapped the piss out of Gayle. Dessie yelled, "I'm sick of your shit, Gayle!"

Gayle was frightened as she raised her hand to protect herself. Never, in their nearly forty years of living, did they physically harm each other.

Dessie fussed, "You act like we ain't been through the same shit! Raped, molested, losing a sister! I will never understand how sisters raised under the same roof become so different! I'm going to raise my girls with pride and dignity. And if I got to wipe down every damn house in Detroit all the way to California, then I will do it!"

"I'm sorry, sister-

"Enough of that sorry shit!" Dessie said, lowering her hand. "I can't live in the past, Gayle. I have to protect whatever I have left."

Three days later, Mama led Erica and me to an apartment complex. As we were led to apartment 812, the stench of smoke filled our noses. Erica sneezed a few times in the old tinted green building, which had peeling paint and was decorated with scribbled wording, profanity, and artwork.

Our apartment had two bedrooms, one full bath, a tiny kitchen, and an attached living room. We were on the eighth floor, and a fire escape was outside the small balcony.

I looked out the window and down the street and saw we were across from a grocery store named Franks. Some homeless people scattered around it, laughing and playing cards on crates. People went in and out of the store carrying bags of goodies and occasionally spoke to each other.

"I'm sorry that it's not a lot, but it's ours for now," Mama said. She pulled open one of the dusty cabinets, and a mouse leaped out and scurried on top of the counter.

Mama screamed, and then Erica panicked. I took off my shoe and chased it around the floor's base and out the door.

"Get out of here!" I said as I chased and tried to beat the mouse. "It's okay, Mama. I can protect us," I said.

I was more afraid of Mama's feelings being hurt than that mouse. I knew she tried to do all she could to be the best mama in the world. She hugged us tightly. Without saying a word, I knew the deep meaning of her gesture. When she hugged me, I felt the strength, courage, determination, and love wrapped in her bosom.

As time went on, we cleaned the place and tried to make the best of it. Erica and I shared a tiny bedroom big enough for two twin beds to be placed across each other. A small dresser we shared was placed in the middle.

I placed Aunt Sweetie's picture on the dresser and prayed that she would visit me in my dreams, but she never did. I stopped asking her and decided to let her rest until she decided to come and see me. I'd wait no matter how long it took. Aunt Sweetie never liked to be rushed or told what to do.

We didn't see another mouse, so Mama had a plan.

"Girls, I have an idea. I'm going to start selling pies to make some extra money," she said. "I can go right to that grocery store across the street and get everything that I need."

And that's what Mama did. She got acquainted with the owner of the store, Mr. Bradley, and purchased everything she needed to go inside of her sweet pies.

Mama also taught us to bake. Erica was too busy studying, so Mama and I were mainly in the kitchen.

"You can't tell anybody the recipe. This is going to be our secret. Do you understand?" Mama asked.

"Yes, I do," I said.

We got the apartment smelling so good that there was a knock on the door. It was an elderly woman, Ms. Collins.

At first glance, I thought she was so sweet and vulnerable. She might have weighed no more than 110 pounds and was in her early seventies.

"I just had to ask what you are cooking that got it smelling so good," Ms. Collins said, putting her skinny hands on her frail hips. "I'm just so used to smelling cigar smoke and old food in the trash can," she said.

"Peach pies," Mama said. She welcomed Ms. Collins inside and invited her to sit on the couch.

"Normally, I mind my business. As you can see, these folks around here can't be trusted. You have such beautiful young girls," Ms. Collins said.

Mama thanked her, and out of the goodness of her heart, she gave her a slice of pie to taste.

Ms. Collins bit into it, and I saw her eyes widen each time she chewed. She shook her head and patted her tiny foot like a church mother.

"My Lord, where have you been? This is amazing! How much do you charge for a whole pie?" she asked, smiling and spreading her wrinkled face.

"Five dollars," Mama said. She winked at me.

"I'll have to tell everyone I know," Ms. Collins said, and she ordered a peach pie for the following day.

Time went on and I spent many hours in the kitchen helping Mama. I was beginning to pour in all the ingredients without using measuring cups because I trusted my guts of when to stop and my heart of when to add more spices.

Since I was terrible at schoolwork, I used baking as an excuse to skip my lessons. Erica didn't bother to learn to bake, but she made Mama a wonderful drawing to advertise.

"How do you like it?" Erica asked.

Mama took the paper that Erica drew on and held it up. "I love it," Mama said, "Dessie's Delights! This is such a beautiful drawing," Mama complimented.

It was a short time before people stopped by to buy a slice or two or a whole pie. Mama only sold her pies on Tuesdays and Thursdays, for she was still working at Ms. Sugar's home throughout the week and sometimes on the weekend.

One night, Mama had only one slice left. There was a knock on the door. Mama opened the door slowly and saw that it was Gayle.

"You forgot you have a sister," Gayle said, stepping inside the apartment. She took off her mittens and stuffed them inside of her purse. "I guess you are doing good for yourself, huh?" She scanned around the apartment and shook her head. "I guess anything for peace of mind."

"This ain't about you, Gayle. But I'm glad to see you," Dessie said. "Why don't you have a seat?"

"I guess I will. How have you been?"

"Working and keeping the girls in school. The normal. Nothing fancy, as you can tell."

"Dessie, come back home with me, please."

"Gayle, I can't. If I go back with you, the girls will have to change schools again. I don't have time for that."

"C'mon, Dessie, you only have one smart-

Dessie snapped her eyes at her and dared her to keep talking.

"What I mean is, it shouldn't be an issue. Dessie, I missed you and the girls. Anyway, do you have any pie left?" Gayle asked.

"I do," Dessie said in a nice-nasty tone.

I placed the apple pie on a plate in front of my auntie. When I handed her the fork, she took my hand and said, "I was once an innocent little girl. My sweet niece pooh, my *Honey*. Did you help your mama make these pies?"

"Yes, ma'am," I said proudly.

"Good, you keep on helping your mama."

Gayle took a bite of the pie and started giggling. "Dessie, you make this pie just like Mama. I swear there is not another fat, Black woman who can cook like you or Mama. My goodness. It reminds me of when we were little girls and we ate at the table, and Mama came over, and she said that you were going to carry the recipe down because Sweetie and I didn't like to cook. Sweetie and I couldn't stand *no damn* kitchen."

"Yes, she did," Dessie said, ignoring her sister's rude comment.

"And, she...now this is really funny. Mama told me... wait for it now, because this will make us laugh, and Lord knows we need to laugh more," Gayle said.

We all giggled nervously and waited for her to tell us what was so damn funny.

"She told me that I was lying about that old man fingering my pussy!"

Her laughter stopped abruptly. We all paused and stared at each other. I was stunned that Aunt Gayle would say something so vulgar in front of us. She really lost her mind.

Gayle swiped her hand across the table, and the plate crashed against the wall.

"Fuck you, Dessie! I miss Sweetie so much. We will never be the same. I should have kept all that money if I had known you would have rented some *stock* pen. You always made dumb decisions, and if it hadn't been for us coming down to Alabama to see you, then Sweetie would still have been alive. Whether you like it or not, I'm the only sister you have left, and you *left* me!"

Dessie stood against the wall and was shaken hysterically. Aunt Gayle made Mama feel guilty, and it took everything in me not to defend my Mama and try to whoop Aunt Gayle's strong-face ass. Auntie felt alone fighting for herself and had nothing to hold on to in the world. Her ass was whooped already.

"I can't do this anymore," Dessie said, shivering. "Gayle, you don't control my life. I love you, but I can't trust you. You get so nice, then you get so mean like I ain't nothing to you but a dog. You always want people to forgive you, but you *never* forgive anybody else." As tears flowed heavily from her eyes, she said, "Thanks for coming to see me, but I have to let you go. Get out!"

"Dessie-

"Get out!"

Gayle looked at the mess on the floor and the crack in the wall she had caused. She realized she had taken it too far. Her reaction was a mistake, and it might have been the last straw that ruined her relationship with the family.

Aunt Gayle took a sad glance at Erica and me. I looked down to the floor, and Erica turned her face away to the wall. We didn't know if that would be the last time we saw her, and we didn't care. We didn't give a damn.

"Clara, I want you to take these pies up to Ms. Collins and come right back," Mama told me.

Mama had to work in the evening at Ms. Sugar's home. We were left with strict rules when Mama was working and Erica was in charge. We weren't allowed to do anything but go to school and come straight home, and if we went across the street to the store, Mama would watch us from the window. The rules didn't bother Erica as much as it bothered me.

Mama handed me the box with the pie. She kissed us and waved goodbye before she headed out the door.

"Come straight back, don't go anywhere else, make sure this door is locked, and be in bed by ten," Mama ordered me. Clara's curfew was at midnight.

Ms. Collins lived on the tenth floor. The elevator wasn't operating, so I had to take the stairs. On my way up, I met a young Black girl easing down the steps holding her stomach. She was crying as she took her time, one tiny step at a time, holding onto the rail. She looked rather uncomfortable. An older lady, who I assumed was her mom, helped her.

"Is she okay?" I asked.

"She's fine," the lady said, without acknowledging me. She was too busy making sure that the girl didn't lose her balance or trip on her black gown.

Once they were out, I headed up two stairs and down the hallway to Ms. Collins' apartment, 1013. Ms. Collins loved to talk, and I knew Erica was timing me, so I sped walked.

I loved talking to Ms. Collins, too. She was rather delightful.

I got to her door and knocked.

"I told you I am done for the day!" Ms. Collins fussed before opening the door. When she realized it was me, she changed her attitude. "Hey, there," she said. "Oh, I forgot that I ordered a pie. Silly me," she said and scratched her gray head.

Ms. Collins reached into her gown pocket and handed me the money in exchange for the pie. She quickly closed her door. For once, she didn't ask me how my day went or compliment me on my hair.

Something was weird about the visit, and something sure was strange about the ladies I met coming up the stairs. I might not have been book-smart, but I had my head in the streets.

I went back to my apartment and looked out the window down the late-night street. I saw all those grown people having a good time. They were dressed nicely, coming to and leaving a nightclub around the corner.

I thought about how the world was out there and how many exciting things were happening. I was tired of Mama keeping me sheltered and away from it all. I was curious, and I wanted to see it for myself. I wanted to know why people acted the way they did. Why do they smoke, drink alcohol, and have sex? It must feel good. It must feel damn good. As far as I know, there wasn't an innocent soul, and I was not interested in being the good girl Mama wanted us to be. I left that good image up to Erica. I had to find myself.

It wasn't too long afterward when Mama would leave for the evening, and I would sneak out of the apartment while Erica was asleep. I counted a few more women passing by, looking distressed within a few days. One girl was as young as fifteen years old, coming down the stairwell as I went up. She looked at me and stared as if she wished to say something. Then, she held her head down and staggered away.

I eased up the stairs and noticed the hallway was empty. So, I pressed my ear against Ms. Collins' door, hoping to discover the mystery that had left me uneasy.

"There's no need to be scared, girl. It won't harm you," Ms. Collins said, irritated and snappy.

"That's right, so you might as well go ahead because I already paid the lady."

I gasped and quickly covered my mouth. That second voice belonged to Aunt Gayle. I wondered what they planned to do to the woman I heard weeping. I could tell on the other side of the door that she was petrified.

"A baby isn't going to do anything but be in your way," Gayle said. "You get this over, and you'll be happy that you did it. Trust me."

"If she doesn't make up her mind in one minute, then she's going to have to go," Ms. Collins said. "And I mean it."

"Listen here, girl. You lay down with that man that you don't know, and if you have this baby, you are going to let him ruin the rest of your life. You'll be forced to remember him whenever you pick it up!" Gayle said.

"This is so hard for me. I don't think it's right," the woman said. "I'm going to leave."

Gayle slammed her against the door. "I already paid her. You ain't got a choice. You are a prostitute, and you are working for me! If you don't go ahead and get rid of this baby, I'll be the one to make sure someone gets rid of the both of you," Gayle said, holding her against the wall.

It was hard for me to grasp the fact that my auntie was one mean bitch.

"You might as well stop all that crying," Ms. Collins said. "C'mon, it's only going to take a couple of minutes. Maybe next time you'll be more careful. Only Jesus can save a whore, but you got to stop sucking dick long enough to pray."

It made sense now. Women were coming to Ms. Collins to get rid of their unborn babies. I began to shake angrily before realizing I had no business being there. It was one part of the world that I wished I didn't know about. I didn't know such a thing, and Ms. Collins was far from a doctor. She was some old lady who was dumber than I was. That old bitch was a bonafide idiot.

My legs shivered as I crept down the stairs. I went inside my bedroom and tried to forget what happened, but it was too late. The damage was done. I wished I'd minded my business.

I realized why Mama kept Erica and me sheltered away from the world. I was sick to my stomach. Those poor women, those poor babies, that evil Ms. Collins and that damn auntie of mine.

SIXTEEN

Maple sorted through her junk drawer in her room and threw away old mail

and papers.

"I don't know why I bother to keep all this stuff," Maple said. She was done cleaning when she told Ivy to come inside her home.

"How's work going?" Maple asked.

"It's going," Ivy said. She acted like she moved mountains instead of dresses. "Mind if I get myself something to drink."

"I don't mind at all," Maple said. "I'm tired of all these dresses I have to make. I have a few more, and I'm done. I promise you that." She sat next to Ivy. "Why are you so looking sad?" Maple asked.

"I'm not sad. I'm just...trying to figure out how I got into this mess," Ivy said.

"I know how?" Maple said.

"How?"

"Being nasty!"

"Ms. Maple!"

"Well, it's the truth."

"But I really thought I was in love," Ivy said, sipping the juice.

"I've been there before, but I still have a little way to go before I meet my first so-called love," Maple said. She sat up and continued her story...

IN 1963-

I was nine years old when I was in my room stitching a dress for an old

doll. I heard Leon calling my name.

"Baby Sis," he said, leaning on the wall.

I stopped what I was doing and gave him my attention. I saw how worried he looked. In his left hand, he held a bunch of envelopes. I tossed the doll on the corner chair. I asked him what was wrong.

Mama was standing behind him, and he turned to look at her as if she was okay with him telling me the news. Mama nodded, and Leon spoke to me in a low voice.

"I have something to tell you, so promise me you won't get upset," Leon said.

I looked at him, Mama, and then at those mystery envelopes that Leon was squeezing.

"I won't get mad," I promised.

"Remember when I told you to never check the mailbox because you never know what may bite you and cause your flesh to crawl and-

"Leon," Mama said, stopping him.

"Well, that's not true. I didn't want you to check the mailbox because I didn't want you to find these letters from...*our* dad," he said, holding his head down. "I was ashamed to tell you, but our dad did not abandon us. And, at one point, I did have a great relationship with him."

I eased off my bed and held Leon around his lanky waist.

"I already forgive you," I said, "Even before you asked. So, what's the truth?"

Leon looked down at me. For the first time, I realized how soft his eyes were, and they glowed like bronze medals.

"He's in prison," Leon said.

I released Leon and saw he wasn't kidding.

"For what?" I asked.

He turned his face and glanced at Mama before he confessed.

"Murder."

I paused. My heart raced as I clenched my chest. I settled myself down to prove that I could handle the news.

"It's okay," I said, "It must have been a really good reason why he killed someone, right?" I asked, hoping that I made some sort of sense.

Even though Dad broke one of the Ten Commandments, I knew it must have been for a good reason. Leon and I were good people, so there was no way we could be seeds of a murderer unless he killed someone because he had to.

"These are the letters he wrote to us," Leon said. "I never read them, but I saved them just in case you wanted to."

I stretched my hands and grabbed the letters from Leon, dumping a pile on my bed.

"Yes, I want to read them and write back to him, too. I don't care what he did. He deserves to hear from his children," I said.

Later in the evening, I sorted the letters by date. Dad had been writing to us for six years, and I had at least fifty letters to read.

I didn't plan on staying up late, but when I started reading, I could not stop. I found out so much about Dad.

I thought he was a prankster. I thought he was Leon's twin in so many ways. But I was genuine like him in the way he loved his Mama. I started crying, and I cried until I went to sleep with the letters all around me.

The following day, I went into the bathroom and washed up for breakfast. I overheard Mama and Leon talking.

"It wasn't so bad, was it?" Mama asked.

"She took the news better than I thought she would," Leon admitted.

"She's a strong, young girl," Mama said, slipping him a plate of pancakes.

"Thank you for not rushing me into telling her," Leon said.

"I knew the time would come, and I'm glad you trusted yourself to wait for it," Mama said.

"Good morning," I said, sitting at the table. I scooted my plate over, grabbed the maple syrup, and poured it all over my pancakes.

"That's enough," Mama said. "My goodness. I know you love *maple* syrup, but it's too sweet, and too much of it isn't good for you."

"Yeah, you're going to have your pancakes swimming," Leon said, laughing at the corny joke. I could tell he was uneasy about last night when he told me the truth.

Mama said grace, and we ate our food. No one mentioned the letters or asked if I started reading them. I found out so much, but I never found out why he would take someone's life. I wasn't even sure if I wanted to know.

After I ate, I rushed back into my room. I wanted to know if Dad would confess. I needed to know what happened to land him in a horrible place. I found out in the very last letter.

Dear Children,

I know I have been writing for years, and still no reply. I hope you read this and find me kind. That would be great. Your grandmother always told me that I was hard-headed and that I never gave up. I always had hope. And for some strange reason, as I write this- I know you got every letter and were ashamed of me. And you have the right to be mad, for what I did was a disgrace. I let the slightest bit of my anger overtake me and messed up horribly. I had kids to raise, and your mom was gone on the other side of Glory. She is dancing in God's Ballroom. That's what we called Heaven 'cause your Mama loved to dance.

Leon, I'm still determining if you'd ever tell Anna what happened and where I am, but I hope you do so. I told you, I always have hope.

So, I will write my last letter to my Dear Anna.

Dear Anna,

You were two years old when I last held you. I remember sitting in your bedroom trying to find ways to make ends meet to feed your chubby cheeks. It was hard, but I knew I had to do something, and praying wasn't getting it done. I tell you, milk was expensive, and as a man, your daddy, I do any means to get it. So, I started stealing. I know it's sad to say, but I would do anything. I'd buy a pack of gum and have the milk tucked under my coat jacket. I ain't no bad person. I had to do what I needed to do to keep you from crying.

I wasn't the only one broke and needed to feed a baby. One night, I left, and I stole some milk again. This time, a man caught me on the side of the store. I knew of him, he stole like I did, but this time, I stole the last milk off the shelf. The man got mad at me and started cussing me out and threatened that he was going to tell on me to the owner. I cussed him back out. We exchanged words for a bit. He told me his son was hungry, and I told him my baby girl was too. I ain't giving up my milk, and he damn sure wasn't going to take it from me.

Next thing, we found ourselves tussling on the snow. I got the best of him and started whamming him on the top of his nose until he bled out. I dusted my pants off and grabbed the milk off the ground. I thought that was the end, until the other man, who I had no clue who he was, stopped me. He pulled his gun out and told me that I better give up the milk. He had a baby to feed, too, but he didn't know I was quicker with my gun than he was with his gun. I drew my gun out and shot him quicker than he blinked his eyes. For the first time in my life, I was terrified and proud. Afraid that I ended his life, but proud because I'd do anything for my kids. It wasn't right, but it was necessary to do it.

I rushed home, cleaned up, and took your beautiful, crying self from Leon's lap. I fed you the milk and watched you fall asleep in my arms. Finally, you were satisfied.

So, I ain't a bad person. I made a bad choice and was too prideful to ask for help.

I need you to write to me so I can keep going and finish this race strong. I can't lose hope, but this is my last letter, and I'll trust God to determine the fate of my story. I love both of you and if I had to, I'd do it all over again. Why? Because I am your Dad.

Always hoping,

Daddy

"Nooooooooo!" I screamed.

Mama rushed into my bedroom and grabbed me on the floor. Leon followed behind her and froze at the doorway.

Mama rocked me and comforted me.

"Are you going to be okay?" Leon asked. "This is my fault," he whispered.

Leon believed he had made a wrong decision by telling me the truth and handing me those letters, but it was the best decision.

I hushed my mouth and wiped my tears.

"I told you he is a good man," I said, "I must write him back. I am his last hope."

My first letter to him was simple and to the point. I was too excited and nervous to think of anything great to write. And I wrote so fast and ugly that I had to rewrite it three times.

Dad,

It's me! It's me, Anna, your daughter! Hey, Dad! Leon said hi, too! I'm 9 years old now, and Leon is 16.

Love you,

Anna & Leon

A week later, we received a letter back. I opened it and saw it was a formal letter. It stated Dad was no longer there. I sobbed, threw the paper down, ran into my bedroom, and crawled under my bed.

"Mama, I told you it was a bad idea!" Leon screamed.

"You better watch your tone of voice when speaking to me," Mama said. She picked the letter off the floor and read it. "They moved him to another facility. This county is actually closer to us. Anna, get your butt in here right now!"

I dried my eyes and walked back into the living room. I was so anxious to get a letter from Dad that I didn't read the entire thing.

I apologized to Mama.

A few days later, we received mail from him.

My Children,

Thank the Lord. I knew God would do it. I miss you two so much. Please, come and see me. Hope never fails!

Love,

Daddy

"Your dad really held on for all those years," Ivy said.

"Yes, he did," Maple replied. She drank her wine and shook the near-empty bottle. She tried to sip every drop of red wine.

"I'll buy you another one," Ivy said.

"Ivy, the story has yet to get good. Go ahead and buy three more."

"Are you sure?" Ivy asked.

"Excuse my language, but the shit is about to get real good."

SEVENTEEN

"Good morning, Tally," Ivy greeted. Ivy was happy to see Tally again, but she did not receive the same type of greeting.

"Good morning," Tally said, barely looking at Ivy.

"Is everything okay," Ivy asked.

"Yes," she said, "I'm glad to be back at work. These new dresses are so ugly."

"Yes, they are. I know a talented lady who can out-design any dress here," Ivy said.

"Who?" Tally asked.

"Her name is Ms. Maple," Ivy said, "Such a sweet lady."

"Yes, she is. She actually designed my dress for the upcoming ball. And she so happens to be one of my older cousins," Tally said, smiling slightly. "And I need you to do me a favor, please. Don't tell her that I'm dealing with my boyfriend. She hates him. As a matter of fact, don't tell her that you know me. It makes it easier. I know Maple is good at pulling the truth out of someone, so please save yourself the headache."

"Why? Ms. Maple is the sweetest-

"Just don't, please."

"Okay, fine. I won't."

"That's Good. Now, let's get to work and figure out how to sell these ugly outfits."

After work, Ivy decided to talk to Honey about Tally. Tally was adamant about not telling Maple about her boyfriend, but she said nothing about not telling Honey or anyone else. For sure, Honey knew what was going on.

"I work with Ms. Maple's cousin, Tally," Ivy said.

"Really?" Honey said.

"And she told me not to tell Ms. Maple about the guy she's dating," Ivy said.

"Oh Lord, don't tell me that she is still messing with-

"Russell," Ivy said.

"Oh, Lord!"

"Ms. Honey, what's wrong?"

"The jackass is an abuser, and Maple told her that she needs to stop messing with him."

"I knew something was strange, but Ms. Honey, you can not tell Ms. Maple."

Honey looked at Ivy strangely and said, "You know damn well we tell each other everything. Is this your way of trying to help, Tally?"

"It is. She's a sweet woman who needs to recognize her worth."

Honey smiled.

"The same thing I need to do, huh?" Ivy asked. "Maybe we can help each other overcome these stupid, no-good men. Brian was a lot. However, he knew not to hit me. Ms. Honey, do me a favor?"

"What is it?"

"Don't tell Ms. Maple what I know. I can get through to Tally. Letting Tally know I was why Ms. Maple found out isn't good. I don't want any tension at work."

"I'm not so sure about that."

"Okay, Ms. Maple finds out she is still dealing with him. How is that going to make it better? Did it stop her from going back with him before?"

"You do have a point. But-

"Let me try to get through to her. I can do it. I know I'm still a mess, but I want to help her."

"Okay, I'll let you have it this time. But if Maple asks if I heard from her, I'll tell her everything I know."

"Okay, that's fair enough."

"Were you always bad at keeping secrets?" Ivy asked.

"I remember the biggest one that I kept from Mama."

Honey got herself comfortable on the couch and told her story.

IN 1968-

"Erica, how many times will you scrub that floor?" Mama asked.

Erica was cleaning the apartment because she invited her boyfriend, James, over to meet us. She made sure there wasn't a speck of dust. She was so nervous that she went back and forth to the mirror, making sure she looked nice.

"You must really like him," I asked.

"Yes, I do," Erica said.

Erica surprised me when she started dating. I thought she was only interested in books and passing exams. I was happy for her. Honestly, I was scared that she would miss out on the best parts of life. Her nose was too stuck in the books.

"For some reason, he really wants to come over after I begged him not to," Erica said. "But I gave in." She shrugged her shoulders and checked her watch.

"Well, I'm glad he's finally coming over to show his face," Mama said.

Mama was as curious as I was.

"Me too," I agreed.

There was a knock on the door, and Erica got frantic. Before she opened the door, she glanced in the mirror again and greeted him with a wide grin.

"Hi, James," Erica said.

I never heard my sister sound so timid and happy.

"Hi, Erica," James said, handing Erica yellow flowers.

"Oh, thank you. Come on inside," Erica said, smelling the flowers and placing them on the table.

James was a handsome nerd. The only thing he needed was a pair of glasses. He was dressed preppy in his white button-down shirt tucked in his blue slacks. His shoes were brown and shiny. I thought he was the perfect match for my sister in terms of his looks. He was about an inch taller than Erica, and they had the same light-buttered complexion.

"This is my mama, Dessie, and my little sister, Clara," Erica said, introducing us.

"Nice to meet you both. I heard a lot about you two," James said.

"Same here. Why don't you take a seat?" Mama asked him.

He made himself comfortable, while I scooted over and eased my way to the corner of the living room. I was careful not to be seen when I smashed a cockroach with my foot. I smiled quickly, and when James turned his head, I kicked the dead bug out of sight.

"Erica told me that you were brilliant," Mama said. Her first impression of James was good.

He laughed and said, "I'm not as smart as Erica, but I do pretty well in school. I'm looking forward to becoming a doctor."

Erica giggled. "We often talk a lot about Biology and how complex subjects can be. James is also a great mathematician who skipped the fifth grade."

"Yes, I'm looking forward to attending an Ivy League school, and I hope Erica will join me. There are more opportunities now for us African-Americans."

This is so boring and cute at the same time, I thought.

"Can you fight?" I asked.

The neighborhood was rough, and I needed to know if he could protect my sister from danger. By looking at him, I was confident that the answer was no. He was too wimpy.

James laughed. "I mean, I can defend myself if I have to."

"Clara, what kind of question is that?" Mama asked, shaking her head at me.

"I'm asking because if something occurred and he had to protect my sister, I'm pretty sure knowing the periodic table isn't going to save her," I said.

I giggled, but I wasn't kidding.

The neighborhood was terrible to the point where I started having fights. Mama would fuss at me, but she knew if I fought, then I had a damn good reason to. I was often teased because I was behind in my schooling.

As for Erica, she wasn't a fighter, so it would have been nice if her boyfriend was rough around the edges.

James cleared his throat and responded with a wise-ass answer. "At the end of the day, fighting is all about balance. No matter how big they are, I can calculate how to throw them off their feet," James said, "also, there are spots in the body that we call pressure points. Pressure points like the Suprascapular Nerves, which are located here," he said, pointing above his collar bones. "Or the wound of the neck, which is located here. You squeeze these parts. Anyone is guaranteed to let go."

"I don't think Clara needs any more ideas," Erica said.

James said, "But you never know when you have to defend yourself. Anyway, Erica, I came over to ask you if you want to go to the school dance with me."

Erica was caught off guard. She acted as if he had invited her to Paris, but it was just a school dance, so I didn't see the big deal.

"Mama, can I go?" Erica asked.

"Erica, of course you can," Mama said, smiling.

Erica went to the school dance and talked as if she had the time of her life. In her long, golden dress, she stood tall and gorgeous. Mama did everything she could to afford the perfect gown for her special night out.

"James and I had so much fun," Erica said, bragging. She got a little taste of freedom and looked refreshed like she had come out from under a rock.

After school, she started spending a lot of time with James, studying and doing what nerdy couples do, I guess. So, she had no time to tutor me, and I was okay with that.

My sister was in love with James. I never knew seeing my sister so elated would make my day.

I knew that I had no interest in anything related to school, so it was satisfying for Mama to see one of her daughters go to a school event.

"I'll see you two in the morning," Mama said. She headed out to work with Ms. Sugar before she gave us the same rules. We were back into our routine of being stuck in the home.

"Erica, do you want something to eat?" I asked. I decided to make a turkey sandwich before I went to bed. Erica didn't say anything, so I went into our bedroom.

Erica was sitting on the bed with her head down, wiping tears off her face.

"Erica, what's wrong?" I asked.

She just sobbed. It was like I was talking to myself.

"Erica, what is it?" I asked.

I sat next to her and wrapped my arm around her shoulders. I figured it had to do with James. James must have broken my sister's heart, and that was the only scenario that came to my mind.

"Did James do something to you?" I asked.

There was no response. She refused to speak to me or acknowledge that I was in the room, but she cried.

"I'm going to call Mama," I said.

Erica put her hands up and said, "Don't."

She looked at me with those puffy, wet eyes.

"Then tell me, what is it? I promise I won't tell Mama."

She sighed and bowed her head down again.

"Clara, I'm pregnant." She leaned over, and her head fell into my lap.

I held her damped face. I was too shocked to say anything. I stroked her hair.

"I don't know what I'm going to do. I ruined my future. I can't go to college anymore," Erica said. "I can't have this baby."

I hesitated on what to say. I stroked her hair a couple of more times.

I whispered, "Don't worry, sister. I know where to take you."

A Few weeks passed, and Mama did not know that Erica was with child. We knew we had to act fast. I needed the money to pay Ms. Collins, and we weren't sure how much she charged, but I knew I needed to give her an amount worth considering.

When Mama went to work, I stayed up all night baking pies and selling them by the slices to the neighbors. I was very sneaky all in the name of helping my sister.

I shopped at Franks, the grocery store, to buy ingredients. I made peach pies because they were my favorite, and people liked them much more.

"Back again," Mr. Bradley said. He smiled at me and rang up my price.

I became a regular there, and Mama had no idea how many times I had been inside that store. I could have probably shopped there with my eyes closed.

"Yes, I am," I said. I paid him and sold him a pie.

I dashed out the door and headed across the street to get home. I needed to make one more pie before I collected enough money to pay Ms. Collins.

"Are you sure you want to do this?" I asked Erica. I removed the pie from the oven and set it on the counter. "Mama and I can watch the baby while you go to college," I said.

"I'm sure," Erica said softly. "Mama has her hands full already, and it wouldn't be fair to you. I worked too hard in school. I want to be somebody. I don't want to be like Mama. I love her, but I can't struggle like her. I refuse to do it," Erica cried.

She was crying too damn much for me.

I didn't say anything, but Erica pissed me off when she said, 'I don't want to be like Mama.' In my eyes, Mama was a hero. Mama was the backbone. Mama slaved so that she could wear the pretty, golden dress to the school dance that made her puny ass so happy. And if she had decided to keep her baby, Mama would have hiked her skirt and broke down bricks with her hands to provide.

How dare she? But I had to respect Erica's decision. A part of me wished I had never suggested she get rid of her unborn child. So, I kept my mouth closed.

Damn, I should have minded my business.

That night, I sold the pie. The next night, when Mama went to work at Ms. Johnstons, whom she called Sugar, I guided Erica to the tenth floor. I grabbed her sweaty palm and told her that she would be fine.

Erica wore a long, purple pajama gown to her ankles. I held her hand until we reached Ms. Collins' door.

I knocked.

"Hey, Ms. Collins," I whispered, hoping nobody saw us.

Ms. Collins quickly pulled me and Erica inside of her apartment. She folded her arms, buried her eyebrows, and asked, "What's going on?"

Ms. Collins knew we were Dessie's girls and was surprised to see the Dessies's girls creeping up to her place in the wee hours of the night.

"Dessie's girls," Ms. Collins said surprisingly. "Okay, who told you two about me?" she asked. Seeing Erica's dress, she knew why we were standing inside her apartment. We certainly weren't coming over to spend the night and have cookies.

Erica looked down at me.

"I found out," I said, "that you like to help women."

"You came to the wrong place," Ms. Collins said. "I need your mama's permission before I do anything."

"Why?" I asked. "Who knows how my mama would feel about you doing this?"

Ms. Collins ain't said anything.

"You aborted a lot of babies, and I need you to do this for my sister, please. She can't ruin her future. She worked too hard," I said, pleading with Ms. Collins. This wasn't the time to show any compassion.

I took out a wad of money from my pocket.

"I can't take it," Ms. Collins said. "Yawl is Dessie's girls, and I can't get myself to do this."

"Okay, fine. We will leave," Erica said. "School will always be there. I had sex, and I need to face the consequences of my actions. I get it."

We turned around to leave, but Ms. Collins stopped us.

"Hold on," Ms. Collins said, snatching the money from my hand. She flipped her tiny fingers through it and stuffed it in her purse.

"If you have that baby, you won't be going to college. You'll find yourself stuck and trying to make a penny stretch into a dollar, and I don't want you to struggle. You are too smart for that. Your mother told me how proud of you she was, and I don't want to see her hurt."

She lit a cigarette and patted her right foot. Her nerves must have been pretty bad, as she was tapping that foot a mile a minute. We were the last ones she expected to see.

"I don't like doing this shit. I hate it. This hurt me every *single* time. I killed a dream, and I created a chance all at once. A chance for a woman to get it right, a chance for a woman to stop being foolish, a chance for a woman to have freedom from abuse as I kill a dream from an innocent baby." She ran water into a pot and turned the stove on. Inside the pot, she placed sharp, silver tools while keeping the cigarette dangling from her mouth. She tied her black, thin robe around her tiny waist.

"But this is how I make my money, and I'd be a fool to let *my* emotions get in the way. Then I'll have to wonder where my next meal will come from. I ought to be ashamed of myself." Ms. Collins walked towards Erica and cuffed her face. "I am going to do this for you not only because I'm pathetic but also because you need this second chance. Please, don't disappoint yourself again. Don't you *dare* be a stupid girl again."

EIGHTEEN

"How's the job coming along," Maple asked Ivy.

"Going pretty good. The styles are not cute, but women are still buying them," Ivy said. "Are you almost done with those dresses?"

"Just a few more to go." Maple rocked back in the chair and crossed her ankles. "I decided to take a rest for today."

"So, did you ever visit your dad?" Ivy asked.

"I did," Maple said, sighing.

We loaded the inside of Mama's old red Buick and headed four hours down the road to see Dad at the state prison. I was anxious and had all kinds of thoughts running through my mind. As Mama drove, I sat in the backseat and barely spoke. I was so in my mind that I didn't hear anything. I knew Mama was playing the Gospel, but I tuned it out with my own prayer.

Mama turned slowly inside the prison entrance, where she had to stop at the guard shack.

"What are you here for?" the guard asked rudely. He did not smile or care about seeing us.

"We are here for visitation," Mama answered. She matched his energy and didn't smile a bit. She was tired from driving and didn't have time for foolishness.

"I.D.," he said.

Mama dug in her purse and handed the man her I.D.

"Open your trunk," he demanded.

Mama opened her truck, and Leon watched the white man. I was scared because of the interaction.

"Go all the way down and take a left," he said, handing Mama her I.D.

"Rude ass," Lean whispered.

I soon forgot about the guard as we approached the building surrounded by a high fence with barbed wire on the top of it.

This was no place for a human, I thought. Why couldn't the judge see that he had great intentions and that he defended himself? Dad was thrown away for most of his life. I soon had mercy for my dad, whom I had only met through a letter. In that letter, I was one with him. I could feel his presence.

It was the longest dirt road on the property before my Mama parked her car where the visitors were allowed.

It was like we simultaneously took a deep breath all at once. I was finally going to meet my dad, Kane.

"Listen, children. They have a lot of rules here. Just follow them. We want a smooth visit," Mama said, and she prayed before we got out of the car.

"These folks are nothing but the devil," Mama said. "I'm not talking about the inmates."

After the guards checked us each, we sat in an open room on bolted metal tables. We sat near the middle of the room, with the four guards standing on the wall, watching our every move. We were not the only visitors there. Other families and visitors waited for their loved ones, too. I could tell some were as nervous as I was.

It was creepy, scary, and nerve-wracking, yet I was relieved to finally meet my dad.

The prison door popped open, and so did my eyes. The prisoners, dressed in orange jumpsuits, walked in individually to greet their family and friends. Then, there was my dad being rolled in a wheelchair by one of the guards. His hands were still cuffed.

He didn't tell me that he couldn't walk.

I knew it was him because he was Leon's twin. He was bald-headed and muscular but shared those same bronze eyes as Leon. I wanted to run and hug him, but I kept my composure and waved frantically. We were not allowed to touch.

He was at the table opposite us and said, "Hey, baby girl! Leon, my boy! Mama Ethel, thank you so much."

Leon wept like a baby. He probably heard Dad's voice more than he saw his face. The tears kept flooding his eyes. It was like Leon had experienced a breakthrough.

"I'm so sorry, Daddy," Leon kept saying. "I miss you."

For years, Leon felt ashamed of Dad for taking someone's life, but I felt courage. I wished he had gotten away scot-free.

I kept my eyes on Dad as he talked, trying to squeeze every conversation he could into an hour. He had a glow in his eyes that I would never forget, and he spoke intelligently.

"I'm good. I'm better. The Lord has been with me," Kane said. "I earnestly waited for this day to come."

I studied his face, and I knew something was wrong. It was as if he had to find strength to keep talking, but I know when someone begged for rest. I thought he was too overwhelmed and not getting much sleep.

"Oh, that's good news," Mama said, smiling and rubbing Leon's back.

Lean wouldn't stop weeping.

I told him all about me and how good I was in school. I told him I loved to sew and hoped he would be home soon.

Leon...he cried.

"It's okay, son," Kane said as he wiped his teary eye.

"I love you, Dad. I'm just so happy," Leon said.

Time flew by, and it was time for Dad to go. The guard grabbed the back of his chair and whisked him away from us. Mama promised that she would take us back to see him.

After the visit, we got a motel room and stayed the night. Mama didn't like to drive in the dark, and for an older lady, she had a heavy foot but bad vision.

I tossed and turned all night thinking about my dad's condition and how he spent the past years caged and forced to be away from those he loved. I couldn't shake the image of him out of my head. That wide grin was stuck in my memory. I thought about how my life could have been with him in it and how his life would have been different if I was never born. Guilt sat in. My dad was inside that place because of me.

I sighed, and when I closed my eyes to sleep, it seemed like it was time to awaken and head back to Detroit.

When we got settled back home the next day, I took out my pen and began to write to my dad. I promised him that he would receive a letter from me soon. I sealed the envelope and placed it in the mailbox, hoping to hear from him.

"Mama, what's wrong?" I asked.

Mama was sitting in front of the sewing machine but wasn't sewing. She sat there blankly and said, "Tell Leon to come."

I ran outside and screamed as loud as I could, "Leon!! Mama wants you!"

Leon hated it when I called his name out in front of the neighborhood to tell him Mama wanted him. So, he wasn't happy when he got inside.

"I told you I hate when you call my name like that!" he yelled.

"So, what?"

"I'll tell you what!"

"Stop it, you two!" Mama yelled. Once calm, she continued, "Promise me, you won't be mad at God."

Leon and I looked at each other and started to worry. It had been a long time since Mom looked troubled.

"I promise," I said. I nudged Leon on his elbow.

"I promise too," Leon said.

"God is still good!" Mama demanded. "No matter what, don't allow the cares of this world to run you away from Him because He is still God!" Mama preached.

"Mama, what is it?" Leon asked.

We weren't in the mood to hear any preaching.

"Did something happen to Daddy," I asked.

I embraced myself.

"This morning, he was found dead in his cell," Mama said. She hurried up and grabbed Leon, but I ran off too quickly for her to comfort me.

I sped to my room, slammed the door, and I cursed God. How dare she tell me not to be mad at Him? Who did she think she was? I was nine years old, and both of my birth parents were gone. I got every damn right to be pissed off. What kind of life was this? God knew he was looking forward to our next visit, and he lived only to see me for an hour since I was an infant.

My face was numb with anger.

Mama opened my door, saying, "Baby-

"I don't want to hear it!"

"You can't talk to Mama like that," Leon said.

I screamed, "Shut up and go away! Leave, now."

I fell to my knees and grabbed my aching chest. My heart had needles dancing away on top of it. Maybe Leon made the wrong decision to tell me that

Dad was around. Therefore, I wouldn't have to endure this unbearable pain. Mama gave me space to grieve. I slept on the floor because no nerves were left in my body. I didn't feel enough muscle to push myself off the carpet.

A couple of days later, Mama handed me a letter. Dad had written to us before he passed away, but Leon and I had separate letters.

Dear Anna,

It was a pleasure seeing you. My heart was overwhelmed with joy, and those chains around me never felt so light. You have grown to be a beautiful girl. When I saw both of you, my world lit up, and I knew what love was. But there was something that I didn't mention because I didn't want you to worry. I am sick. Very sick. I was told I only had six months to live, but I told God to keep me here until I saw my children. And that's what He did. I know, baby girl, I had your hopes up, but I'd rather fly high with God and look down on you. I am going to be free soon. So, don't be angry.

I'm so glad that you two are in Mama Ethel's care. She is a woman of God and one who has faith. I wouldn't want anyone else to raise my children but her. She knows the Lord. So, listen to your Mama so that you can have a prosperous life.

Anna, I hope you cherish every waking moment of your life. I hope you find in your heart to make peace that I fought hard only to be reunited with the ones I care for the most, my children.

Love,

Daddy

P.S. The hope now lives within you!

NINETEEN

"Look at the independent woman," Brian said sarcastically when he saw Ivy going to Honey's house. "Still living with Ms. Honey. It won't be long before she has enough of you, too."

Ivy ignored him. She was too tired to respond and feed into the games that he was playing. His antics were getting outdated.

"Hey, Ms. Honey," Ivy said, entering the living room. She took off her shoes and sat on the sofa.

"How was your day?" Honey asked.

"Is it Friday yet," Ivy said. She was ready for the weekend.

Honey laughed and took the pies out of the oven. Her Godson, Marcus, would pick one of them up soon.

"Did your mom ever find out about your sister?"

Honey shook her head and said, "No. Erica and I promised to keep that secret and take it to the grave. It was hard. I look back and thank God my sister didn't get too sick."

"Whatever happened to Ms. Collins?"

"Passed away with guilt, but Erica and I were long gone from those apartments when she died. She lived to be ninety-four, I think," Honey said.

Honey looked down, saddened.

"Ms. Honey, what's wrong?"

"I'm getting closer to when Mama is ready to say goodbye forever," Honey said. "God, give me the strength."

IN 1969-

"Mama, are you okay?" I asked.

Mama kept no secrets from us. A few months ago, Mama sat us down and told us that she had breast cancer. The news shaped the course of our lives. It was painful to see Mama endure so much and still try her best to provide.

I was fourteen and flunking out of school, and when I heard the devastating news, I nearly wanted to drop out and take care of Mama. We prayed every night before we went to bed. We sometimes believed in the good news.

Mama prepared us for her transition. She encouraged Erica to finish school and attend her dream university. Erica knew she was bound to get a scholarship. As for me, Mama told me about housekeeping jobs.

I wasn't worried about my future. I wanted Mama to survive, but Mama's appearance changed drastically. I knew she was Mama, but I barely recognized her. Mama stopped working and relied on what she had left in her savings, which wasn't much.

Mama visited her sister, Gayle, during her last days.

"No, no, no," Gayle said, refusing to accept Dessie's fate. "You can't leave me. I'm not going to have a sister," she cried.

"Gayle, look at me," Dessie said. "I need you to be strong and listen."

Dessie reached into her pocketbook and pulled out a checkbook. "I didn't use all the money you gave me from the land. I left most of it to my girls, and I left some for you," Dessie said, handing her the check. "I have enough money to be buried and-

"I do not want to hear this." Gayle got up from the table and walked over to the window. "Dessie, why are you giving up? Isn't there still a chance? Can you fight a little bit more for me, please? I know I did shit that wasn't right, yet you turn around, and you treat me so good. *I* deserve to bear your cross. *I* don't deserve to be here," Gayle said, shaking her head.

Dessie left her seat and placed their mother's pearl necklace in Gayle's hand.

Gayle twirled the jewelry with all her fingers. "We should have buried Sweetie wearing this. I ain't getting married."

"Then give it to one of my girls," Dessie said. "I need you to lift your head and push. You're going to be a mother. You are about to see what it's like to have a life bigger than your own."

"I don't know anything about being a mother."

"They are going to need you. Erica is going off to college, and Clara—she's a fighter. I haven't worried much about them. I taught them all I could. Now, I need you to cherish what you have left."

"Mama was gone," Honey said, wiping her tears. "She left us on an early Sunday morning. I'll never forget. I was on Mama's right side, and Erica was on her left. We cleaved to her hands. The hardest thing we ever did was give Mama the permission to leave. She fought hard enough."

"I had four hundred to my name and a mean-ass auntie, who I couldn't trust. Erica had gone off to school, and I dropped out. The world Mama shunned me away from was the world that I had to embrace. I had to survive it. And to do so, I turned into a heartless, bitter woman. I turned into the woman I despised the most, my Aunt Gayle."

There was a knock on Honey's door. It was Marcus. Marcus ran to Honey, hugged her tightly, and said, "I love you so much, Ms. Honey! You mean the world to me."

Life knew Honey needed a warm embrace to comfort her after years of missing her mama. Honey smooched all over her Godson's face. It took some of the burden away.

Marcus' mother, Brandy, was a lady whom Maple and Honey helped get on her feet. Brandy wanted to have an abortion when she was pregnant with him, but Honey convinced her not to.

Brandy had said, "You must be going to help me take care of him."

Honey said boldly, "Yes, I am! I'll do anything for you to keep that child."

Honey grabbed hold of Marcus and said, "Oh, I love you too!"

TWENTY

"You sure you don't want to go to the ball," Maple asked Ivy.

"I don't have anybody to go with," Ivy said.

"Then, go by yourself. You don't need a man to have a night out."

Maple was cleaning her work area when Ivy stopped by to chat. Maple was nearly done with all of the dresses.

"Have you ever gone to the ball?" Ivy asked.

"It's nothing fancy for me. I wasn't worried about a ball when I was your age. But it does remind me of the time Leon went to the prom...."

IN 1966-

"Well, look at how handsome you are," Mama said when she saw Leon coming into the living room.

Leon stood proud in his black tuxedo and red vest. Nobody could tell Leon's ass a damn thing about how good he looked. He kept smoothing his hair with his hand and licking his lips.

"Thank you, Mama," Leon said. "Thanks for letting me borrow the car to pick up Clarissa."

"Looking great, bro," I said, "and I have something for you,"

I handed Leon a red and black handkerchief that matched his outfit. I sewed it together and decided to surprise him on prom day.

"Thank you, Baby Sis," Leon said, and he hugged me.

"That's so sweet of you," Mama told me. She handed Leon the keys to the car and told him to be careful.

"I will. I'll see you tonight."

I watched Leon from the window as he got into the car and drove off. I couldn't wait for my big day. At least, that's what I told myself.

Mama sat at the kitchen table and opened her Bible. She would take her left hand and scan the words while her other hand held the handle of the cup filled with hot tea. She studied the Bible religiously. Sometimes, I would join her and ask her questions about God. Who was He? Why does He allow bad things to happen to good people? Does He really send people to Hell? Is God really coming back? What does He sound like? I hammered Mama with questions, and she would give me an answer that made me go awe.

"I hope Leon has a good time," I said.

"Knowing your brother, I'm pretty sure he will," Mama said, laughing. She closed her Bible and looked at me.

"What's wrong?" I asked.

Mama had a look of concern on her face.

"You remembered when we talked about the seasons of life?" she asked.

"Yes," I answered.

We usually have Bible study on Wednesday nights, but something weighed heavy on Mama's heart. She gazed around the house as if everything were meaningless. Glancing at Grandpa John's photo in the corner, she looked at me and held out her hand.

Mama said, "There's a time to be born, and there is a time to die."

"Mama, no!" I said. Somehow, I knew what she meant. I was sitting on the edge of my worst nightmare. Not *you too*, Mama.

"It's going to be okay, baby. You will go through some things in life, but if you and Leon stick with God, then you two will be okay. This isn't my home, and it isn't yours, either," Mama said sternly.

I hated it when she preached terrible news and found good in it. I said nothing because I was too busy fighting back my tears. My head felt like a bucket filled with water as I held it in and puffed my cheeks out.

Mama was old, and I wanted her to send me off to prom like she did Leon, but she was too busy believing in Heaven. How did she know she wouldn't be just sleeping, and God wasn't waiting for her or anybody else in the sky? I wanted to debate Mama, but I clenched my jaw. She reminded me that one day, when I leave this earth, I will hurt someone, too.

Mama began to sing, *"If you live right-*

We used to sing that song almost every morning. It was our favorite tune, and we harmonized so well that I nearly got caught up.

I refused to sing. I looked at Mama and shook my head slowly.

"If you live right," Mama sang, looking for me to join her. "Come on, girl," she said. "Let me hear that pretty voice."

Mama sang, *"If you live right-*

I wiped the snot from the top of my lip.

"Heaven belongs to...you," I sang, weeping.

"If you live right-

"Heaven belongs to you."

"Heaven belongs to you," we sang one last time.

"My sweet baby, God got you!" Mama said.

"I'm sorry, Ms. Maple," Ivy said.

"Don't be. Mama prepared me for a lot of things. I had no idea what she was talking about, but when I got older, I understood. When Mama died, I was so lost."

"But you found your way back," Ivy said.

"Yes, I did. But it was a hell of a journey. Ivy, it's time to get to the real good shit. I'm going to make your ass look like a saint."

"Let me go grab some wine."

"Ivy-

"Ma'am-

"No more wine, we *need* Gin."

TWENTY-ONE

Ivy was proud of who she was becoming, but there were some kinks that she had to get rid of. She knew that there was no such thing as perfection, so she slowly worked to forgive herself. She wrote down the things that she was grateful for and proud of. She envisioned her life, realizing that she was capable of true love. She even read a few scriptures in the Bible.

As she wrote, she thought about her dream job, husband, and what she hoped to accomplish within the following year. With a stroke of a pen, she poured into herself everything she wanted. When she finished writing, she closed her journal, meditated on her thoughts, and said a small prayer.

She checked her phone and saw a text from Tally. Tally also agreed to the self-healing challenge, and they decided to hold each other accountable. Ivy replied, *yes, girl, I just finished writing. How about you?*

Tally responded, *Thanks for putting me on this challenge. I do feel relieved. #Girlpower!*

Ivy smiled and was glad she was making a friend around her age. No disrespect to Ms. Honey or Ms. Maple, but she needed someone that she could relate to. Women desire to be loved and be loved in the correct way and for the right reasons.

Ivy decided that she was going to take a nap, but she heard Honey opening the front door.

"May I help you?" Honey asked.

Honey had no idea who the lady standing on her porch was. The woman was fair-skinned, tall, and clutched her purse under her arms.

"I'm Nora Hutchins. I'm looking for my daughter, Ivy."

"Mama," Ivy said.

Ivy was surprised that her mother traveled from North Carolina to check on her. Ivy stood behind Honey and wished she could have hidden. She never expected her mother to travel hundreds of miles and pop up on her.

Honey politely moved out of the way and welcomed Nora inside her home.

"Well, nice to see you too," Nora said.

"I'm Ms. Honey. Come in and have a seat," Honey said, guiding Nora into her living room.

"Ivy, I've been worried sick about you. Did you think that I wouldn't come to see you?"

"How did you know where I was?" Ivy asked.

"You sent me your fiancé's address a few months ago," Nora said, sitting. "I found it mighty strange that you've ignored me for the past weeks. Usually, we would talk on the phone for hours, but you have been cutting me short. So, tell me, what's going on?" Nora asked. She cleared her throat, waiting for Ivy to answer her question.

"What exactly do you know?" Ivy asked.

"I went to your fiancé's home, and he told me you were here with Ms. Honey. That is all I know, but- I have an inkling feeling that something else is happening."

"He said nothing else?"

"Why would he say anything else? Ivy, what's going on?" Nora asked impatiently.

"Brian and I are no longer together," Ivy said quickly.

Nora looked at Ms. Honey and knew there was more to the story. "Ms. Honey, are you a mother?" Nora asked.

"I am. Two sons."

"I'm sure you would know if your sons were lying."

"Of course I would."

"Ivy, there is no way you have avoided me because of a breakup. Spill it," she said.

Honey nodded, meaning she needed to go ahead and confess what had transpired between her and Brian.

Ivy sighed and said, "Brian is a married man. I knew he was married, but I believed he would somehow want to be with me. That's why I've been avoiding you, ashamed of my behavior. He eventually got rid of me."

Honey looked at Nora and waited for her reaction. Nora sat back and crossed her legs before she spoke.

"Your father was married when I met him," Nora said, shuffling her shoulders.

Honey thought, *What the hell?* She leaned back in her chair and crossed her ankles, so surprised that Nora bragged about being with a married man too.

"Mama!?" Ivy gasped. She was shocked at her mom's proud response.

"Yes. I wasn't going to allow that fine man to get away. Your daddy is six-four, has good credit, and brought in more than six figures a year. Back then, that was good money. The difference between you and me is that my plan worked. I can't say I'm proud of what I did because I put up with a lot of shit afterwards. Excuse me, Ms. Honey, for my language in your home. But don't trap yourself like I did, Ivy. You make sure you live independently so you don't depend on a man. Brian would not treat you like you deserve anyway with that small house in this mediocre community. But, Ms. Honey, your house is beautiful."

"No offense taken," Honey said, giving her a faint smile.

"So, do you even love my dad?" Ivy asked.

"I do, sometimes. I know I can't sustain myself without him, and that's not a good place to be. I got everything I wanted, but I lost my voice and my backbone. I sit back and take things I know weren't fair because I never had enough means to leave. You don't want to live that life. So, when are you coming home?" Nora asked.

"I'm good here," Ivy said, "I have a job, and I'm getting on my feet."

"Good, but if you need anything, please let me know," Nora said and stood up. "Come and give me a big hug." She whispered in her ear, "There is nothing you can do that will stop me from loving you."

"Thanks, Mama. I love you."

"How about dinner tomorrow night before I leave?"

"Sure."

As soon as Nora left, Honey grabbed the phone and called Maple.

"So, the mama is a whore too?" Maple asked, laughing. "Poor Ivy couldn't stand a chance. What did she look like?"

"She looks like one of those old Hollywood women. I knew she had some work done on her face because her eyebrows wouldn't raise worth a damn. I think she was more disappointed that Brian wasn't a millionaire."

"Isn't that the truth," Maple said. "Ivy should feel better knowing where she gets it from."

Later that evening, Honey and Ivy were in Honey's bedroom. Ivy drank so much red wine she almost forgot she had work in the morning. She nearly passed out on the comfortable chair.

"That wasn't as bad as you thought it would be?" Honey asked.

"No, but it was very interesting."

"I can tell you one thing for sure, a mother's love is special. When my mama was gone, nobody knew anything about me. I had to find myself, and well, that was a mess....that was a complete *damn* mess.

IN 1975-

"Clara, how was work?"

Aunt Gayle asked me when I arrived home from working at Mr. Walter's Diner. I was a waitress there, and I would bake pies there when I felt like it.

I remember coming home, and Aunt Gayle was drunk. I knew it. And the reason why I knew she reeked of alcohol was because it was a Friday night. She stayed drinking, but those damn Friday nights were the worst.

"It was fine," I said, picking up bottles off the table and throwing them away. I decided to clean the bottles off the table before I swept the mess on the kitchen floor. I hated living with Aunt Gayle, but that was my only choice. She was the only family member I was taught to know.

"Did you find that pearl necklace?" Gayle asked, checking under the couch pillows like it would magically appear in the same spot.

Every time she got intoxicated too heavily, she would bring up the pearl necklace.

I hadn't seen that necklace in over three years, and I believed Aunt Gayle sold it to pay a bill or to buy liquor.

"No, I haven't," I said. I gave up looking for it. It nearly broke my heart that something so valuable was no longer in the family.

"You talked to your sister, Erica?" Gayle asked, sitting wide-legged on the stained, toffee-colored couch, scratching her head and fanning herself. She stayed hot and sweaty.

"Yes, she is doing good," I said.

"That's good. She was the first of the family who graduated high school and took her ass to college. Shit, I finished the tenth grade, and your Aunt Sweetie was the dumbest. Shit, I think Sweetie finished ninth grade, and your poor

Mama, she ain't had a chance. Shit, she had two babies by the time she was seventeen. Erica's big head ass, and then you come bald-headed since you were four years old. We never thought you would grow any hair. We, the Brown's Sisters, had some pretty hair. Yes, we were some pretty women with fluffy hair. You sure as hell got the look now. It makes me proud that *one* of the two looks like us."

I learned to ignore her ass. I let her continue to ramble on while I cleaned the pile of plates that filled the kitchen sink.

"Did you find that pearl necklace?" Gayle asked, checking under the pillows of the couch again. "Erica, she will graduate and get her name on that paper. What do you call that shit?"

"A degree," I said.

"I've got my name on a piece of paper too. I've got my name on these damn bills." Gayle picked up the envelope.

"I paid the light bill," I said.

"Good. I was wondering." Gayle stood up. "I know you had a long day. So, I made you something." She walked towards the kitchen and opened the refrigerator. "I made you a pie."

The pie looked awful and undone. It was messy. It looked like someone had crumbled brown, thick glue and spread it on the top of cherry blood.

"I know I ain't you, and I know I ain't Dessie," Gayle cried. "But I tried. I tried to make the pie all pretty, but the motherfucking pie wouldn't bake worth a damn!" she yelled and leaned her back on the wall. "Maybe, maybe it's not as bad as it looks. Do you want to try it?"

"No, Aunt Gayle. I am fine," I said nicely, trying not to hurt her feelings.

"Are you sure? Maybe it's not that bad. It looks bad, but it's good, like me. I know I look like shit right now, but I'm a good woman. Can't nobody tell me that I ain't no good ass woman!"

As I listened to her, she started talking out of her mind, trying to console herself. I never attempted to validate her feelings because the next week would be another drunken episode.

Aunt Gayle dipped her finger in the pie and licked it. Her mouth quivered as she held her stomach to lean over and vomit in the trash can.

I grabbed Aunt Gayle by her side and helped her into the bedroom. I laid her on the bed and handed her a wet towel to wipe her mouth.

"Go to bed, Auntie," I said softly.

"You hate me, don't you?"

"Get you some rest," I said. *Hell yeah, I hate you*, I thought.

I closed the door and continued to clean the mess she made. I secretly wished she had stayed asleep forever. I was so tired of her, but I had to protect what was left, and sadly, it was her.

Some time passed, and things got better because Aunt Gayle was back in the streets. She was bearable as long as she had a man and some money. I would come in from long nights working at the diner, and she would be leaving for longer nights with a man. That was fine with me. I would keep the home tidy and invite my boyfriend over. His name was Daniel, and he took my virginity. Shortly after he lay with me, Daniel avoided me. He was the first man who left a hole in my heart.

I started drinking heavily to deal with it. I gave my innocence to him, only to have him treat me like shit. I began emptying out my auntie's bottles of alcohol to ease the shame.

Mama taught me about boys years ago, but I threw everything out the window to satisfy my flesh. What hurt me the most was not following Mama's advice.

"Have you been drinking my shit?" Aunt Gayle asked. She decided to confront me one night. I guessed the man had left her alone.

"Yes, I have," I said without any hesitation.

If auntie had caught an attitude, I was willing to fight her ass that day. I was heartbroken and used to it, and I didn't have time to put up with her anger. She wasn't the only one going through bullshit.

"Clara, you are not supposed to be drinking. You are still a teenager. You mess around and get hooked, and next thing you know-

"You become a whore," I said, looking dead at her.

I didn't know if the alcohol made me brave or if I was fed up with her trifling behavior. She kept inviting strangers into our home and allowed them to raid around naked and fuck anywhere.

She wagged her finger at me and said, "I can't wait until your ass gets out of my house."

"For what? You can't survive without me. I help you pay every bill in this stinking house. Just because you can sell your ass, it doesn't make you grown, *auntie!*"

"You sound just like your mama."

"Do not you bring my mama into this. Aunt Gayle, I will hurt you and never look back! I swear I will."

There was no point in keeping peace with an addict. I stayed quiet long enough. Auntie didn't take hints too well that she was selfish and cared nothing about my sacrifices as a young teen who was forced to survive off broken scrapes and form a way of living.

"I'm going to let your hot tale have that. Hmm, but when life hammers you down and-

"Fuck me!" I yelled. "Life had been fucking me for the past five years, and when life fucks it fucks hard and long, but when a man fucks at *least* it *can* feel good. And when that man leaves you, you have to deal with the fact that life is still fucking you, and *life* doesn't care if you're sore. *Life* does not care if you bleed out! *Life* doesn't whisper sweet things in your ear. NO! It just pounds away at you until you find something else to ease the pain, but *LIFE* is still there, waiting to creep back in after you settle down from your high that will never last long enough to ease the pain. Now, ask yourself, do I sound like my mama?"

TWENTY-TWO

"Hey, Ms. Maple."

"Hey, Ivy. I thought you put me down," Maple said.

"I took on extra hours at the boutique. Are you done sewing those dresses?"

"Not quite, but I'm done for the day." Maple stood back and was impressed with her work. "Do you have any plans for the weekend?"

"No plans."

"So, you still enjoy listening to two old ladies telling all their damn business," Maple asked, smiling.

"I can listen to you and Ms. Honey all day."

"Good. My childhood stories are over. Now, you are about to hear from a grown-ass woman....

IN 1973-

"That got-damn, Richard Pryor! I tell you, he is one funny

man!" Leon said, watching TV and slapping his thigh. "Ain't

nothing funnier than a nigga telling it like it is."

"That's all you do is sit around that TV," I said, picking my afro and twisting and turning in front of the mirror. I was wearing my bell bottoms and multi-colored tank top.

"My ass works hard. If I want to watch TV all day and drink my beer, let me. And where the hell are you going this time of night?" Leon asked.

He muted the TV.

"Why don't you mind your business?" Clarissa said, coming out of her bedroom. "Your sister is grown. She's nineteen."

"Tell him again, sister-in-law. You don't need to worry about me when you have all these children running around here. You have one more child, and he's going to be sleeping in the kitchen."

"It wasn't my intention to have four children-

"Five," Clarissa interrupted, rubbing her stomach.

"That's because you can't stay away from me," Leon said. "But as your brother, Baby Sis, I gotta keep you safe. That's what I promised Mama."

"I'm grown as hell, can't you see."

"I'm seeing too much if you ask me. Why don't you cover up some?"

"She looks fine the way she is," Clarissa said.

"Stay out of this, Clarissa. We weren't raised to be acting like this and going out and-

"No offense, but you had three kids out of wedlock," I interrupted.

"So what? I don't need you to have any. So, where are you going?" Leon asked seriously.

"I'm going to the Tavern tonight, me and some of my girlfriends," I said, grabbed my purse, and headed out the door.

Leon caught me by the arm. "I don't like that place. Niggas act like they ain't got no sense there. You have no business being at a place like that, and I know Gloria fast-ass is going, too. She ain't your friend, Baby Sis. Why don't you do some regular shit like go to the movies or the mall in the daytime?"

"Leon, I just want to have fun. I know how to protect myself, and I'm certainly not going to do anything stupid."

I looked at his hand around my arm so he would let me go.

"You have to trust her," Clarissa said.

Leon sat on the back of the couch and shook his afro. His sister was no longer that little girl he once knew. I had a mind of my own. Leon checked his watch and saw that it was almost 9:30 that night.

"I tell you what. I'm going to start putting these babies to sleep, and if you aren't back home by the time the last one goes to sleep.... then I'm coming to you. Now, Junebug is hardheaded and fights his sleep, so you will have plenty of time to have your fun."

As frustrated as I was at Leon, I couldn't help but love him. He always looked out for me. I gave him a light kiss on the cheek and told him that I would be fine.

I arrived at the Tavern and got-dammit, I had the time of my life. My girlfriend Gloria and I danced the night away. Nobody could tell me that my ass wasn't big the way I jived on the floor. Men were constantly pulling at me and offered to buy me drinks. I turned them all down. I had no time for a man. I had dreams of moving to LA and becoming an actor. I wanted to be the next

Dorthy Dandridge. If not an actor, then a Hollywood stylist, dressing them for the red carpet.

It was nearly two in the morning, and I was ready to go home, but Gloria wasn't. She was stone drunk and acted foolish, flirting with men provocatively.

"Girl, what are you doing?" I asked.

I searched everywhere for her. I found Gloria behind the club talking to some guys. She was sloppy and stuck between them, barely standing as she smiled with her eyes half-open.

One nigga lifted her breast, and the other nigga rubbed up her thighs. I knew she was in trouble, and she was my ride home.

"Gloria, it's time to go," I said.

Them niggas looked at me crazy. I started to run to the nearest pay phone and call Leon, but I refused to leave Gloria. I knew those guys were going to rape her.

"Hey, this is my friend, Anna. Anna, this is-

"Gloria, let's go." I went to grab her hand, but one nigga grabbed my wrist and pulled me into his chest.

"C'mon, lil' mama. You don't wanna have some fun?" he asked.

I struggled to get away as he forcefully held me against my own will. I managed to knee him in his nuts and took off running. I guess Gloria snapped out of it a little because she tried to leave, too, but they held her hostage.

"Take that bitch back in!" The man demanded his friend to drag Gloria to the back of the bar. Gloria's weak body could not overpower the big man, who took her back to do God knows what.

I ran off screaming for help, passing people who did not give a damn about me.

"Anna!" Leon called out. He exited his vehicle and met me halfway in the dark alley.

I crashed into Leon's chest, and he asked what was wrong with me. I told him what happened the best I could because I was too terrified to get my words out correctly. He shamefully looked into my eyes and shook his head.

"Hey," the nigga said, pointing his gun out.

Terrified, I threw my hands up and begged the man not to shoot, but Leon took no chances. Leon drew his gun out and shot him before I blinked my eyes.

"Let's go!" Leon grabbed my hand, and we ran to his car. He quickly sped off.

Leon cursed me out. He made me feel like shit.

"We left Gloria," I said, trying to get him to shut up. It was hard to speak when Leon was upset.

"I don't give a damn about Gloria! I told your ass about this damn place-

"But-

"Shut up, Anna!"

I knew he was pissed. He always called me Baby Sis. I sat on the passenger side crying as Leon continued to press hard on the gas and called me all types of names.

He parked in the driveway.

"Was the shit worth it? Ever since Mama died, you act like you lost your damn mind. We will go into this house and act like nothing ever happened. Did you hear what the fuck I said?" He sounded like a Baptist-cursing preacher. I sat in the passenger side of the car and listened like a young girl forced to follow his teaching.

"Leon, what if he died?"

"Then the nigga is just dead. I took a vow that I'd do anything to protect you. Now, I'll let you sit out here to dry your tears because I don't need Clarissa to know anything."

Leon didn't show a lick of compassion. I hated that he loved me so much.

"What happened to the guy?" Ivy asked.

"He barely lived, but Leon was charged with attempted murder," Maple said, crumbling a piece of fabric in her hand. "The judge gave Leon twenty years. His kids had to grow up without a father because of me. I couldn't deal with the guilt for a long time, and honestly, I still have a *hard* time. Daddy went to prison because of *me*, and Leon went to prison because of... *me*. I felt like I was a problem. I felt like I should have never been born."

The phone rang, and Maple answered.

"Baby Sis!" Leon said.

"Hey, Leon. How are you?" Maple asked.

"I'm good! I'm coming to see you soon. Why are you sounding so sad?"

Without saying another word, Leon knew what was aching his Baby, Sis.

"God is good, Baby Sis. Don't waste another hour feeling guilty about the past. Do you hear me? Now, open up this door."

"Say what?"

"I'm outside your house. Now open up this door!"

"Leon!"

Maple was so glad to see her not-so-skinny, bald head, brother with those bronze eyes. She had to remind herself that they were not young anymore, so she was careful not to knock him down when she embraced him, sobbing on his shoulders.

TWENTY-THREE

"I'm so glad that Leon came to visit, Maple," Honey said, taking a pie out of the oven. Honey was working on some new orders. "Is everything going okay, Ivy?"

"Pretty good," Ivy said.

"That smile is getting brighter," Honey said.

Honey remembered the first time she met Ivy and how she acted. Now, Ivy was changing for the better. She had a new glow on her face.

"Ms. Maple was so happy to see Leon," Ivy said. Witnessing Leon's surprise gesture warmed her heart and gave her hope.

"You have to love people while they are here," Honey said, placing a pie in the oven and setting the timer. "Well, by the time I finish this story, that pie should be ready."

"Hey, Clara," Gayle said.

Aunt Gayle was on the sofa half-asleep.

When I worked until the closing hour, I always brought her a plate of fried chicken and mashed potatoes with gravy.

I had an eerie feeling that she was drinking herself to death. I hated her choices, but I loved her enough not to see her waste away. She lost half of her weight, and her hips drew in. The only thing that stayed with her was her fluffy hair. Other than that, she didn't resemble the Brown sisters.

"Why don't you get in the bed?" I asked.

When I turned around, Aunt Gayle was sleeping, snoring lightly. I figured that I better not bother her. I was too tired, and my feet ached badly from standing all day and walking two blocks to the house. I wanted a hot shower and my bed. I gently threw a blanket over my auntie to cover her exposed boob that slipped out of her shirt.

I opened my bedroom door and pulled out my dresser door to get some night clothes. I raised my head up and glanced into the mirror in front of me, and was horrified to see a naked black man standing behind me.

Terrified for my life, I screamed, "Get the fuck out of here!"

He laughed wickedly, "Come on, now, baby. She's asleep," he said, twirling his big black dick with his right hand.

"I ain't your got-damn, baby," I said. I threw a radio at him and drew an umbrella to protect myself. I held it sturdy in the air and was ready to knock his brains out. It was the only thing I had to keep the sinister away from me.

Unafraid, he licked his lips and grit his teeth, rubbing his right hand over his sweaty body while playing with his erect penis.

"Aunt Gayle! Aunt Gayle!" I screamed.

I just knew she didn't hear me. Aunt Gayle would sleep through a storm.

I swung the umbrella and hit him. The second time I hit him, he snatched the umbrella away and forced me down on the bed. I kept fighting and twisting my body as he grunted and wrestled with me. I managed to dig my fingernails at the bottom of his neck.

"Got- dammit!" the man screamed, letting me go.

Before I could push him off of me, Aunt Gayle sliced him on the back with a butcher knife. Then, she clashed a glass beer bottle against his head. The man was knocked out, bleeding from his temple. Blood was on my bedroom sheets and the carpet.

"Don't you ever mess with *my* family!" Gayle screamed.

I imagined her to be a lioness protecting her cub by the way she roared with her mouth and buried her eyebrows.

I kept looking at the man on the floor. He was naked and wounded, lying on his stomach. I breathe heavily as I try to gasp the trauma of seeing the deeply sliced open wound on the man's back. I trembled in fear and realized that Aunt Gayle saved my life.

"Look at me, Clara!" Gayle demanded.

I looked at her as she held that bloody butcher knife firmly in her right hand.

She said, "I did a lot of shit in my life that I wasn't proud of, but this one I am! Your mama told me to protect whatever I had left," she said sternly. "And that's what the fuck I'm going to do."

Gayle turned into a sweet and compassionate auntie, the one I loved, the one I hadn't seen in a long time when she cried, "But I need you to do me a favor. When I'm dead, don't you dare remember me. Do you hear me? You remember your Aunt Sweetie and your precious mama, Dessie. But please, forget about me. I ain't no good woman to be looking up to."

We hugged as if the butt-naked man wasn't dying in front of us. It was a strange yet beautiful moment between us.

How could I forget Aunt Gayle after she did this for me?

"I'm so sorry for everything," Aunt Gayle said.

We saw the slightest ounce of life when the man wiggled his fingers. It pissed Aunt Gayle off.

"I'm so sorry," Gayle said. She gently moved me out of the way.

Aunt Gayle crawled on the floor, held that butcher knife high in the air, and-

"*Aunt Gayle, NO!*"

She stabbed him to death.

"I ain't sorry no more," Gayle said.

Ivy sat with her mouth open.

"Killed the man right in front of me. I went to live with a good friend until I got on my feet. Aunt Gayle did *no* prison time. It turned out the man was a wanted fugitive and a serial rapist anyway. Aunt Gayle damn near died a hero."

"What happened to her?"

"They said she was sick. I say it was a broken heart," Honey said and paused. "Just like a blink of an eye, three queens were gone. Looking back, only God kept my mind."

The timer on the stove beeped.

Before Honey stood, she noticed Ivy sitting in a daze. "Are you okay?" she asked.

"I can't believe you and Ms. Maple went through so much," Ivy said. She had no idea that their story would be so deep.

"It's easy to tell you what they did, but wait until you find out what *I* did. Ivy, I might make you pack your bags and run you out of this house."

TWENTY- FOUR

"How's the job going?" Maple asked Ivy. Maple was in good spirits after Leon's visit. Her brother helped her take her mind off of things.

Leon had said, "God got Jasmine, and everything will be fine."

Maple teased him and said that he sounded like Mama.

The week flew by. Before Maple knew it, Leon boarded the plane and promised to return. Maple knew Leon would be back as long as God didn't stop him.

"The job is going pretty well," Ivy said. She was at Maple's house to help her organize some fabrics. "I can't believe that you are not in stores."

"Well, I ain't caring too much about that," Maple said. "I work hard enough as it is. I think it's time for us to take a break."

Maple placed a shirt inside a box before taking a seat to catch her breath. With Ivy's help, she finally saw some form of organization in her guest room.

"What happened to you when you left Leon's home?"

Maple looked at Ivy and shook her head.

"Chile....*chile.*"

IN 1976-

"Catch her! Catch her!"

I was downtown running. I was so scared of what happened that I didn't bother taking off my heels. I hurried down the street, running away from a fat, bald-headed man. I promised him sex. I snatched his wallet out of his back pocket and took off. When I turned the last corner, I stopped and caught my breath.

I took the scarf off my head and stuffed it in my purse. I loved luring men in and stealing from them when I could. It gave me a sense of power, and when I saw that they were vulnerable, I did everything I could to humiliate them.

I opened his wallet halfway down the street, only to find twenty dollars.

"What the hell," I said.

The only thing I was able to get was a damn rib plate if that.

"Hey, Dave. You know what the hell I want," I said.

I took a seat on the bar stool. I used to eat for free, but I didn't want to cause Dave to lose his job.

Dave was a cook and my roommate. He let me live with him for a bit, and Dave was one of Leon's best friends.

"Hey, Mr. Almore," I spoke to the owner, "with your fine, old self."

"Hey, there, Anna," he said, shaking his head. "Hurry up and make your friend her order," he told Dave.

"I'm on it," Dave said.

"Are you trying to rush me out of here?" I asked, messing with Mr. Almore.

"I just don't want any trouble," Mr. Almore said, and he threw his hands up.

"She ain't going to be any trouble," Dave said, sliding me a glass of coke. He whispered, "Anna, I think they heard about you robbing men, and you know-

"What are the men going to say? Are they going to say that I denied them sex? Hell, half the men are married or have good jobs. If they tell on me, they would ruin their lives too."

Dave leaned back and said, "Let me make sure your ribs are well done, and I'll add a side of fries and collard greens."

"Add me a pecan pie," I said. "I'm feeling mighty sweet." I took out my cigarette and began to smoke it while I waited for my food. "I can't wait to suck that bone dry," I said loudly.

Mr. Almore heard me, and he shook his head. I had fun picking with him because I knew he was a saved man. He was pleasant, too, and he never tried me. Treat me well? Yes. Hated me? No. Did he feel sorry for me? Maybe so. Mr. Almore was someone who the world needed to be. He was soft, caring, and minded his damn business.

"Here's your plate," Dave said. "What's wrong?"

I lost my appetite. That happened a lot. I would be fine one moment, then the next moment, I felt like shit. Something as simple as a meal would make me feel like I didn't deserve anything in the world. I pushed the plate back and asked Dave to put it away, and I would eat it later. I nearly had to starve and force myself to eat.

"Hands up! Hands up!"

I looked around and wondered who the fuck the police were looking for.

Shit, I threw my hands up, and they tried to arrest me.

"Got-dammit, I didn't do anything!" I said, "You got the wrong one."

"Anna Washington," the cop said.

"What the fuck do you want?" I said as the police held my face on the counter and handcuffed me.

"You don't have to hold her like that," Mr. Almore said.

The cop scurried through my purse and took out my ID. Then he lifted me up to reveal who I was.

"I know who the fuck I am," I said. "Let me go, now."

The cop looked at Dave and smiled. I knew then that they knew exactly where I was going to be, so it only made sense that Dave had told them.

"Dave...Dave, do you know him? You snitching motherfucker. How dare you?"

"I'm sorry, Anna."

"Sorry, my ass!"

"Let's go," the police said, and he escorted me out the door.

"Dave, why did you do that to her? You should have told her to leave if you didn't want her to stay with you," Mr. Almore said.

"She stole from me, Mr. Almore. Anna is turning out to be a wild woman. Anna and her brother were not raised that way. I did everything that I could have done but to steal from me. No, I can't take that," Dave said. "Besides, she's a prostitute."

"I ain't stole, shit. Stealing from a friend is something that I'd never do," I said. "As good as Dave has been to me, I would never stoop so low to do such a thing," I told the booking officer at the county jail.

"You will have to tell that to the judge," he said, handing me a paper with a court date on it. "Good news. This charge is a Misdemeanor, and it is a release of recognizance. Just get your fingerprints, information, and picture, then you are free to go."

I sat in that cold room filled with other criminals, mad as hell. I thought about how to kill Dave before the court date. I was pissed. I was sure it was one of his girlfriends who stole from him. Shit, Dave was a whore himself. The bastard accused me because he cared about what other people thought of him. Fuck other people.

"Washington!"

I got up and walked towards the guard. I looked at him, and we noticed each other. Officer Rogan was one of my clients. He pretended as if he didn't know who I was, knowing damn well he did. Knowing damn well, I *rocked* his world in the backseat of his truck a few nights ago.

I whispered, "I'm impressed by how you can tuck that big thang in those tight pants."

He tried to ignore me. He grabbed my hand to take my fingerprints. He breathed in heavily, and his hands trembled. He was afraid that I would cause a scene. He instructed and guided me by maneuvering my fingers one by one on the ink. My presence made him hesitate and rethink how he was supposed to do his job.

He peeked around the jail to make sure no one heard me.

"I thought you said no hands," I whispered.

"Maple, listen," Officer Rogan said, "I am at work. You don't know me, and I don't know you. Now, let me take your fingerprints so you can leave."

"When are you coming to me again?" I asked.

"Maple, stop it, please."

He took my other hand.

"Don't stop, baby, please," I whispered.

"Listen, I am taking your fingerprints incorrectly. This means your arrest record will not be shown in the future," he whispered.

He showed me how he barely smudged my fingers on the sheet.

"This is the least I can do, so please keep quiet," he said nervously.

I knew his real name and where he worked, so he needed to keep his promise, or else I would make sure he lost his job.

I wiped my hands and took a seat on the chair. I crossed my legs like the baddest bitch in the room. I was going to get my revenge on Dave.

I was released and started walking towards the nearest motel. I heard a car honk at me.

"I ain't working tonight," I said without looking back.

The car horn blew louder, and it irritated me.

"I'm not working tonight, you horny bastard!" I screamed before I realized who it was, Mr. Almore.

"Get in the car, Anna," he said, talking plainly as if nothing was exciting.

I swallowed my pride and got my ass in his car. I was too tired to lie and say that I was okay. I figured I better do what he said so I could take a hot shower and have a roof over my head. I needed rest. I needed to be rescued.

We said nothing on the way to Mr. Almore's house. When he parked, he said, "Come on inside and make yourself comfortable."

I stepped inside his little, cozy two-bedroom home, which was simple and plain, like him. He handed me clean towels and told me where I was going to spend the night.

"I got your clothes from Dave," he said, pointing to the corner of the living room. My belongings were placed inside trash bags and one small suitcase.

I rummaged through my things and pulled out a pair of pajamas.

"There's no need for you to go around, Dave. I don't need you in any more trouble," Mr. Almore said. "Your plate is in the refrigerator. I know you ought to be hungry."

I knew I was a complete mess. I knew I had to turn my life around, but it was easier said than done.

I cried in the shower. I wanted my family back. I was drifting away at sea, and there was no anchor to hold on to. Life was strange and unpredictable. Mama, where are your prayers?

When the morning came, I refused to eat the food Dave had made, so Mr. Almore fried us eggs and bacon. He was off on Sundays, so I learned a lot about him. He was never married and had no kids, but he had his fun 'back in his day.' In his words, "I never got caught up." We laughed.

There was something special about the old man behind the counter at his diner. His calm voice soothed me, helping me find some peace in my chaotic world. He moved as if he had another life ahead of him.

"Mr. Almore, it is very kind of you to allow me to stay with you. But I'm going to have to get out of your way," I said. "You know my life, and you know what I do."

He looked at me like I was a daughter he never had. He wished he could swift me away from the life of prostitution and robbery. He wished he could provide more for me, but the truth was, his diner barely provided enough for him to live on. Some wishes do come true, and some wishes are bullshit. Trying to save me was complete bullshit.

"I'm sure it's something else you can do," Mr. Almore said. He handed me a newspaper to take a look at the job listing.

I politely pushed the newspaper back and explained, "I don't like to answer to anyone."

I hated people who fixed their mouths to tell me what to do. Mr. Almore, who was an entrepreneur, knew what I meant.

"I'll tell you what," Mr. Almore said. "I learned long ago to catch the fish and allow God to clean it. If you ever find yourself needing a place, I'm here."

"Thank you, Mr. Almore."

Two months later, the court decided to drop the charges that Dave had filed against me. He had no evidence, and he had nothing worth stealing anyway. Now that the charge was behind me, I felt like a free woman. However, I was not done with Dave.

I continued to be a sex worker and roam the streets.

One night, I stopped by Mr. Almore's house because I needed a pinch of normalcy. I was tired of fighting with the dangerous game. I refused to end up like Gloria, who was murdered.

"I fired Dave," Mr. Almore said. "Turns out he has a drug charge." He giggled. "People must learn to sweep around their own front door."

I smirked and acted like I knew nothing about it. I had one of my Johns set him up, and it worked perfectly.

I knew in my heart that I was one bad-ass woman. The woman who sought revenge and couldn't rest until something was done. I had zero remorse.

"That's what happens when you don't show people any grace," Mr. Almore said. "I still can't believe he lied about you."

"Life works in mysterious ways," I said.

"Anna-

"Yes, Mr. Almore," I said as I read a book with my feet resting on a stool in his living room.

Mr. Almore paused before he said anything else, so I read another paragraph of the book. I almost forgot he called my name.

"Would...would you think any differently of me if I wanted to have sex with you?"

I closed the book and sat up in the chair.

"I'm sorry," he said. "I know it's weird coming from an old man who loves the Lord, but I...*I*... I've been so lonely. I'm so sorry to offend you," he said, holding his head down. "Lord, forgive me," he whispered. "I allowed my flesh to take control."

I knew he was ashamed of asking me. I was younger than half his age.

"I think you should just go, Anna."

"No," I said softly. "Mr. Almore, you should not be ashamed of yourself. You are a man, and it's natural to have those feelings no matter how saved you are. I am not embarrassed, and neither should you be."

I got up and sat next to him on the couch. I grabbed his hand.

"I just haven't touched a woman in years because I said I was waiting on my wife. I'm seventy-two years old, and I'm not even attracted to women my age," he said.

I laughed and said, "Mr. Almore, you are a good-looking older man in great shape. I'm sure you will sweep a younger woman up quickly."

I felt sorry for him. I couldn't imagine living so long without anyone to love on.

"I don't think so. My face is kind of sagging a little, and-

I kissed his cheek.

"Anna-

"*Shhhh*," I said, "call me...*Maple*."

I stood up and seductively danced for him, taking off my shirt slowly to expose my breasts. I rubbed my breasts and teased him, placing my finger in my mouth and moving my hips. He sat and allowed my seductive spirit to take over him. He submitted himself to what he really desired. His eyes glowed with desire as he looked me up and down.

I was completely naked as I danced slowly and teased him, making him feel young again. I crept towards him and sat on his lap. I placed his hands over my breast, then I lowered his hands to cuff my soft, round ass.

I whispered, "It would be such a shame for a good man to die unfulfilled."

"You married Mr. Almore?" Ivy asked in shock.

"Yes, I did," Maple said. "I loved him. He made me feel protected."

"So, what happened next?"

"His restaurant burned down, and we lived off the insurance money. A year later, he died, and all that was left was mine. That's how I was able to survive a little."

Ivy looked at the clock and saw it was nearly midnight. She wanted to hear more of the story but had work in the morning.

"Ivy, wait until you hear about my second marriage," Maple said.

TWENTY-FIVE

"Maple told me that she told you about her marrying that old ass man,"

Honey laughed.

Ivy found a bottle of red wine.

"I was too shocked," Ivy said. "Speaking of marriage, when did you find love?" Ivy asked, handing Honey a wine glass.

"That would be much longer down the road," Honey said. "I was too busy finding myself."

IN 1980-

"Clara, you're late. You're always late," Walter said.

"What are you going to do, fire me?" I said.

I was always tardy for work and didn't have a care in the world. My attitude gave Walter the blues, but he knew my pies kept customers returning and asking for more. I was the main reason his ass was making money.

"They keep asking for Honey," Walter said. "We don't serve any honey. We ain't got nothing to put honey on. Then I realized they were asking about you," he said, folding his arms. "Where does *that* name come from?"

"You can't tell I'm sweet," I said. "And honey needs to be served with those dry-ass biscuits."

"Clara, when are you going to make those pies?"

"I only make them twice a week. I ain't doing more than that," I said, and I meant it.

I walked past a group of men who were seated at a table.

"I'll be right with you, boys." I flirted and walked behind the counter.

"Hey, Clara," Jo-Ann said. She was nineteen and Walter's niece. Jo-Ann was from the South and always smiled. She was cute—charming but ditsy.

"Hey," I said.

I always tried to avoid Jo-Ann.

I tied my apron around my waist and grabbed my notepad and pen. I went over to the men and took their orders as we laughed and had short conversations. I knew I was bound to lure one of them in and service them later that night.

"Call me, Honey," I said. I could always tell which one of the guys would give me the special attention I desired. It was in the eyes. I made eye contact with one of the gentlemen and winked at him. He smiled and sipped his juice. I was so good at my job that I could tell by what a man ordered that he would be willing to pay for sex.

"How do you do that?" Jo-Ann asked.

"How do I do what?" I said.

"Be so confident. Those guys really admire you," she said slowly in her southern accent. "I was scared to see a bunch of men. They are acting like hound dogs."

"Good. Keep it that way," I said, wishing she'd stop talking to me.

"But, I want to become good like you are," she said. "I would love to get some advice."

"Why do you want advice from me? I'm not that much older than you," I said. "Besides, don't you want to become something more than a waiter?"

Hell, I hated my job.

"Yes, but you carry yourself like a real grown woman," Jo-Ann said.

"But deep down inside, I wish I was a little girl in pigtails sitting under my mama's arms," I told her. She was shocked at my response.

I saw one of the guys staring at Jo-Ann from afar. He was one of those cheap bastards. Jo-Ann looked down and started fidgeting with her apron. I knew she was uncomfortable and tried to be someone she wasn't meant to be.

"Where are you from, and how did you end up here?" I asked.

"I'm from Tupelo, Mississippi. Have you ever been there?"

"Why in the hell would I ever go there?" I asked.

"Well, it is home of the hot Honey. I might have figured that's where you got your name from," she said, smiling. "Anyway, my mom and I weren't getting along well. She tried to baby me and tell me what to do. I had enough of it. I wanted to become a grown woman, so I left and never looked back. My Uncle Walter was kind enough to let me stay with him," she said.

"Do you want my advice?" I asked seriously, hardly paying her any mind.

"Yes, of course."

"Take your ass back home to Tupelo and apologize to your mama. And you *better* keep your ass in Tupelo, do you hear me? All your mama was trying to do was protect you and keep you away from these no good, foul niggas. If you stay here, these men will eat you up and spit you out. No offense, *Jo-Ann*, but you are kind of silly. You're beautiful but weak-minded and very gullible. There's no way in the hell you can make it here. *Jo-Ann,* I may make this shit look easy, but deep down inside, I have no choice but to be strong. I'm only trying to survive. *Trust me*, this is not the life you want."

Jo-Ann stood in silence. She never guessed that I wished I was in her shoes. She had a mama that she could cleave to. I had nobody.

The only thing that genuinely made me smile was hearing from my sister occasionally.

"I don't have enough for a bus ticket," Jo-Ann said.

I snatched the money out of my bra, and I slapped the cash into her hand.

"Take your ass back to Tupelo, and don't look back," I demanded.

"Is everything okay?" Walter asked.

"You're going to need another waiter. Jo-Ann is going back home to Mississippi," I said.

"Jo-Ann, when were you going to tell me?" Walker asked.

"I just found out," Jo-Ann said.

We said goodbye to the last customer and cleaned the diner. Walter made it his business to thank me and paid me for the week.

"I'm sure glad that you were able to talk some sense into Jo-Ann," Walter said. "I knew this wasn't the place for her. Thank you."

"I didn't give her a choice," I said.

"So, I'm down one waiter. What time are you coming in the morning?"

I smirked. Walter knew that I came to work when I wanted to, no matter how much he fussed. Since I did feel a little bad about him being short-staffed, I smiled and said, "On time."

"Good. Whatever time that is, that is good enough for me."

I grabbed my coat, headed out the door, and headed towards the bus stop. "Clara-

I turned around and saw a man—the same man I had served earlier. I told him, just like I told everyone else, that my name was Honey. How the hell did he know me? I had only seen him once. He was polite and tipped me well, but I knew there was something odd about him that I could not place my finger on.

I stepped a foot backward and watched him stop moving forward.

It was cold and dark. I was tired and this man I didn't know, called me Clara.

"My name is not Clara," I lied. *Because who are you,* I thought. "You have the wrong person. I don't know who Clara is."

"I don't think I have the wrong person," he said, pausing before asking, "Is your mama's name Dessie?"

I tried to study his face under the pole light, but he wasn't familiar looking at all. My mama never brought a man around, and I never knew her to date anyone besides Mr. Mogan.

"Who are you?" I asked. I was more angry than scared about this stalker who approached me. I placed my hand in my purse and was willing to tase him.

"I'm Lawrence....I'm your father—

"Step the fuck back!"

"I'm sorry! You look like Dessie to me. I'm sorry I bothered you, but it was worth trying."

"You hid out and waited until I left work to follow me and ask me who I am and if I knew Dessie. You are a creep, and I need you to stay away from me before I blow your got-damn head off." I bluffed, knowing I didn't have a gun.

I walked away. I wasn't sure if I would ever hear or see from him again. If he was indeed my father, he did not deserve to be in my life. *However,* he deserved to feel my wrath if he was my father. He deserved to share my pain. I could not allow my emotions to get the best of me. I had a change of heart. I wanted to know the truth for myself. I wanted to see the truth rather than for a happy story.

I turned around and confessed, "Yes, I *am* Clara– how would I believe you are my father?"

He damn near cried when I told him the truth. He understood I would not jump for joy because I had no clue. I never knew his name. I never asked. I never cared. He was always dead to me.

We talked on the phone for about a month. Lawrence knew my entire family, including when Erica was born. I was convinced to take a DNA test, and the truth was revealed.

One day, I was at his home, sitting before him. I dared not call him dad, although he was my father, according to blood. He was Lawrence—a fat, ugly man named Lawrence. Thank God we had no resemblance. *Thank God! Thank God! Thank God!* I could not thank God enough.

At the kitchen table, I asked for a hot coffee. Lawrence poured me some and placed a mug in front of me. He had no idea of how much I despised him. I smiled in his face and waited for the perfect timing to go in for the kill.

"So, Lawrence. How was your relationship with my mother?"

"Oh, it was sweet. Absolutely pleasant. We fell in love and-

"Why did you leave her?"

"Well, we were so young. We didn't know what we were doing. She already had a child, then you came along. I wanted to stay, but I was a child too. I had to move with my parents to New Jersey. My parents refused to believe that I was the dad. I had no say in the matter. I was a young coward. I hope you will forgive me."

"So, it was your parents who denied you from having a relationship with me. Is that what you're saying, *Lawrence?*"

"Yes, unfortunately so. My parents didn't believe in having children out of wedlock. Very religious," he said. "And by me being young, I didn't think for myself. I hate I had to go-

I pulled the cup of coffee towards me.

"Are you sure it wasn't because you *raped* her?"

"No, no, I didn't rape your mama. Did Dessie tell you that? I wouldn't do such a thing. Where did you get that from?"

I tightened my hands around the mug's handle.

"So, my mama lied?"

Lawrence's fat neck got sweaty, and he hesitated to answer. He looked at me, sitting cross-legged and twirling a spoon in my hot coffee. I got his ass right where I wanted him.

"I just don't know where you got that from. I never never raped a woman in my life. I wouldn't do such a thing."

"My mama said you raped her. That's how I was conceived."

"That's simply not true."

"So, you're telling me that my mama lied."

"I think it's time for us to continue this later—I have somewhere to go."

"Yes, Hell is waiting for you!" I said.

I dashed the coffee on him, then I pulled out a knife and slit the right side of his big face. "You raped my mama, you bastard!" I kicked him on the floor. "Tell me the truth, or I will kill you!"

"It was so long ago," he cried.

I grabbed his shirt and held the knife to his neck. My strength surprised me the way I held him up. I dared him to lie again. He trembled, burning and bleeding. He deserved that pain and more.

Twenty-five years later, I was going to get revenge for my mother.

"I'm sorry," he said. "I was young and stupid. Please, don't kill me," he begged, crying.

I let him go and shoved him to the floor.

I left scared as shit. I didn't know if Lawrence was going to survive.

When I came into work the next day, it was slightly busy. I got the word that Jo-Ann was on the bus headed back to Mississippi. I hoped life treated her well.

I was shaken about the encounter with Lawrence. I did not know if he was coming back for revenge.

I worked hard that night and picked up the slack. It was near closing time when I looked up and saw Lawrence coming into the diner with a thick bandage on the left side of his face. He sat in the corner and took his hat off. I did brutal damage to him.

"I'm so sorry about last night," he whispered. It pained him to talk.

"How can I help you?" I asked.

"I deserved what you did to me."

"How can I help you?" I asked again. I pretended that I didn't know shit about last night.

"Why would you pretend to accept me and you didn't? You knew the truth and pretended to not know. You lured me in and scarred me for life."

You scarred my mama, I thought. I had no sympathy for him.

"You need to order or get the fuck out," I said. "Walter!"

"Oh, Walter knew. Walter was *there*—Walter told me who you were."

"What's going on, god-dammit?" Walter asked, looking at Lawrence, who had a half a grin on his face. "Lawrence, what the hell happened to you?"

"She knew, Walter. Dessie didn't keep a secret like you thought she would. Walter, you told me that I needed to let Clara know who I was, and all along she knew I did a terrible, unforgivable thing. But did she know you helped me do it?"

"Clara, that ain't the truth!" Walter said, "All you do is tell lies."

"Oh, that's some bullshit!" Lawrence screamed. He held his sore face. "You gave the girl a job here because you're *guilty!* You felt sorry because she lost everybody—but you can do nothing to make it up."

Lawrence drew a gun from under his coat and pointed it at Walter and said, "Tell the truth, or *you* die. I ain't gonna be the only one living a secret life."

Walter put his hands up.

I felt sick to my stomach. Two terrible, deceitful villains were at each other, and Lawrence had the upper hand. I wanted both of them to die. Just leave me alone. Just let fate have its way. I backed away slowly towards the exit as they confronted each other.

"Listen, Lawrence," Walter said. "I've got no time for foolishness. Put the gun down, and we can talk about this."

"Tell the *fucking* truth!"

"I had nothing to do with it!"

"Yes, you did!"

"Please, don't make me do this," Walter said, trembling. He looked at me and said, "Clara-

"Clara, how else would I have known where you were?" Lawrence asked. "You made me look like a fool once. You will not make me look like a fool again! So, why don't you tell the truth!"

"Lawrence, I knew you for years, and I know we can get over this if we-

Lawrence shot Walter twice in the chest.

I witnessed him fall backward to his death. I thought I was next, but he placed the gun down and fell to his knees, crying. He surrendered and waited until he was under arrest.

"Justice was served. I went home, kissed my mama's picture, and slept like a baby."

TWENTY-SIX

"I want to say that I am sorry for what I did. You did not deserve that," Brian said, standing over Ivy and caressing her shoulders after they finished making love.

Ivy was hesitant to come over, but she was willing to hear what he had to say. It wasn't long before their clothes were off as they had sex, listening to slow R&B jams.

"Will you forgive me," Brian asked.

"I wouldn't allow you to make love to me if I didn't," Ivy said, bending her neck back so Brian could place a kiss on her lips.

"Do you still wish to marry me?" Brian asked.

"Of course. Now, you must get rid of that wife. And I wouldn't mind helping you to get rid of her if you know what I mean."

"Good. I knew you would be back," Brian said. He placed his hands around her neck gently, and then suddenly, he turned into a madman, choking her. "Bitch! You thought you could live without me!"

Ivy fought for her life, but Brian had a tight grip around her neck, squeezing her to death. She tried to scream, but tiny squeaks creeped out as she struggled to escape. She felt herself going out of it.

"Ivy!" Honey called.

Ivy woke up frantically and tried to catch her breath.

"You are having a terrible dream," Honey said.

Ivy was relieved that the dreadful nightmare was over. She grabbed her chest to feel her rapid heartbeat.

"Thank God," Ivy said. She dared not to tell Honey what her dream was about.

Later that day, Ivy went to Maple's house.

"I hope you aren't giving up on love," Maple said as she watched Ivy looking sad in the living room.

"The hell with love," Ivy said.

"I know it's too early to drink red wine, but I made us a glass of mimosa. I leave all that cooking to Honey. I do enough with my hands as is."

Ivy laughed and took hold of a glass.

"So, what about your second marriage?" Ivy asked.

"Oh, shit. Here we go...."

IN 1978-

It was daylight, and I was downtown, minding my business. I decided to do a little shopping and treat myself to lunch. I heard a man say, "Hey there—I say hey, hey...

I heard his feet rushing towards me.

I thought it was another fool and I was right, but I didn't know it then. I was about to curse his ass out and let him know that's not how you get a woman's attention. But I was happy to turn around and see he was Josea, my first crush.

"Do you remember me?" Josea asked, smiling.

He was looking damn fine. For the first time in a long time, I got shy. I was that little girl standing beside Mama outside the market.

"Josea," I said.

"I haven't seen you since you were a little girl. You and your mama always came to my dad's fruit market on Saturdays, and I'd always save the best fruit for her." He smiled. "Your mama was a lovely woman."

"Well, I ain't no little girl anymore."

And Mama is not here to rebuke me, I thought.

I leaned into his open arms to greet him with a warm hug. I desperately wanted to cling to his back muscles as my ear pressed against his chest. I felt so comforted *and* horny.

"I see, you're mighty grown. Where are you headed?"

"To get me something to eat. I'm not too sure what I want."

"Well, how about I treat you?"

"Fine with me."

He took me to a local Mexican restaurant where he knew everyone. We barely settled into the restaurant when he shouted, "Cumo estan, hijo de puta?"

Everyone turned and looked in our direction, laughing. Josea was well-loved and a big shot. He led me to my seat and pulled the chair out for me.

"What did you say? What was so funny?" I asked.

"Oh, nothing. I asked how these sons of bitches were doing," he said, laughing. "These are my good amigos. We joke a lot."

"Quein es Ella?" the waiter asked, grinning.

Josea answered, "This is Anna–

"Hola."

"Hi," I said.

It wasn't long before we ordered our food and got acquainted.

Meeting Josea was a dream come true. I was infatuated as we spoke over margaritas, and I learned a lot about him. Josea grew up poor and hated working at the fruit market. But his dad wanted an honest living, not the route his drug-dealing uncle took.

Josea promised himself that he would not live in poverty and wanted more in his life. At that moment, I loved his ambition, not having a clue how far he was willing to go to obtain the lifestyle he desired.

When his dad got sick and passed away, he sold the fruit market. He became an owner of laundromats and invested in small businesses throughout the city.

The small chat subsided, and we cut to the chase. We delved into what we really wanted.

"You are gorgeous," he said.

I blushed at him.

He smiled.

"Well, we are both grown now," he whispered. "Quiero que seas mi amante."

I didn't know what he said, but it turned me on.

"It means I want you to be my lover," he said, looking at me deeply in my eyes.

"Si," I said, giggling and wishing he would just take me away and rip my clothes off. I waited for what seemed to be a lifetime to taste his lips.

He laughed, too, and grabbed my hands. I gasped. And a little later, my fantasy was fulfilled. Josea took me to his home, and we had sex. *Mind-blowing sex.*

A year later, we were married. I became Anna Perez. A newborn woman who lived a life of luxury. I woke up in a six-bedroom home with a two-car garage and a backyard pool. Life was great, but it was a dangerous game. Every damn day I heard him threaten to take someone's life if a deal went sour. He was a fool, and I submitted to his will, knowing that the hustle game was eating him alive.

I became unhappy but had no choice but to live with him. I was a former prostitute who spent many nights sleeping on the streets. Now, I was tucked away in satin sheets. Why in the hell would I go back? I believe Josea was the answer. I made Josea my God.

Around two years into the marriage, I gave Joesa everything he desired, including having other women join us in the bedroom.

He accused me, saying, "You're making love with her better than you're making love to me!"

Josea was jealous of Bernadette. Bernedette was more than a menage a trois. She was a sensitive, caring woman who listened. She was someone that I confided in. It was safe to say that I was falling in love with her, but Josea tore her away. He threatened her and told her to never come back because she was ruining our marriage. The truth was, she was the one holding us together. When he separated me from her, it was like my world fell apart. I became invincible, and no amount of sex or money was making me happy.

Josea came home and threw a whole damn rage. He lost money—he lost his damn mind. A drug deal went terrible. He slammed the door into the bedroom, knocking a picture frame off the wall.

"Seems like I have to take matters into my own fucking hands!" he said, pacing back and forth. "Merida! Merida! Merida!"

Bullshit, he loved to say when life angered him.

I watched him take the gun out from underneath the bed, and I knew then Josea was in deep trouble.

"You are not capable of taking a life," I said. "I put up with a lot of shit, but I will not be with you if you decide to do something *so* stupid! Why can't you stop before it's too late?"

"It's not that easy, Anna. It's never that easy. Look at the life I gave you," he said. "What are we going to do?"

"Start over," I said.

"With nothing—I can't go back to nothing. You are my wife, and I need you to trust me. Anna, you must be able to defend yourself if you have to."

He took the gun and placed it in my trembling hand. I never held a gun before, and I knew how it ruined my dad and my brother's life. I placed the gun on the dresser and walked toward the other end of the room.

"You have to protect yourself, Anna–

"Josea, what did you do?" I asked, crying. "I will leave you before I place my life in jeopardy."

He grabbed me and placed me against the wall. He begged me to stop being scared and that somehow, he would make it right. He made it clear that I was not leaving, but I did not want anyone else to be killed because of me.

Josea let me go and said, "Lo lamento."

He was sorry.

Reality struck me harder than any blow a man could give. The fact was that I was still a prostitute, just a married one. I exchanged vows to be committed to a man of greed and deceit. How could he tell me to trust him and then give me a gun to protect myself?

Josea stabbed people in the back so that he could remain on top. I, however, forfeited my soul to stay underneath him to gain fortune.

I looked at him and said what he wanted to hear, "I trust you."

I kissed him and ran my hands down his shoulders to his forearms, where I saw he was injecting heroin into his veins.

His lean body grew faint as he slumped to his knees. He promised me that he wasn't going to be a drug user. He was not supposed to take it this far. He wept in guilt.

I said, "Te amo pero esto demasiado para mi. soy una mujer débil."

I let him know that I loved him, but I was a weak woman.

I wanted to abandon Josea, but our souls were yoked together with the spirits of other women who were invited into our bedroom. I battled with many personalities and insecurities, which I never had. Amid everything, I lost myself *and*...I found out that I was pregnant.

I gave birth to Jasmine on August 18, 1981. She was beautiful and healthy, but postpartum depression hit me like a son-of-a bitch.

I felt like I did not deserve to be a mother. I fought daily to convince myself that I was good enough to care for her. In my mind, Jasmine did not deserve me. Just days before I found out I was pregnant, I had a plan to take my life.

I thought being a mother would give me something to look forward to, only to feel the opposite. I was too dirty to be a mother of such an innocent soul. Jasmine cried a lot, and oftentimes I would scream to the top of my lungs, "Got dammit, what do you want me to do?"

"Is everything okay?" Ms. Holcomb asked, coming into my bedroom.

Josea hired Ms. Holcomb as a maid to help me deal with the stress of becoming a new mother. Ms. Holcomb was patient and assured me that this, too, would pass. She was a grandmother and raised plenty of children. Sometimes I forget she was a hired maid the way she comforted me during my most difficult moments. She helped ease the burden a little, but I was still emotionally drained.

Josea was always away. He was always focused on making more damn money and running rapidly around town.

I looked at Ms.Holcomb, and I burst into tears. I really wanted to love Jasmine, but I was emotionally drained. Tired. Scared. Lonely. Defeated. Trapped. Abused. Yes, Josea was physically violent towards me.

Ms. Holcomb knew about me, and what I was experiencing, so she never judged. She picked up my baby, and Jasmine stopped crying almost instantly.

I felt like shit, and I wanted the feeling to stop. On top of everything, the arguments with Josea were endless.

"What the hell are you doing?" Josea asked.

"I'm packing up my shit, and I'm leaving," I said, stuffing clothes into my luggage. I needed to get away.

"What about the baby? Are you stupid? You can't just leave!"

"Jasmine will be with Ms. Holcomb. I need a break, Josea! You have barely been around since the baby was born. Josea, I don't have anyone! I stayed in this house all day and night, looking at the walls and losing my mind. You keep everybody away from me! You think I'm supposed to be happy because you're making all this money. I deserve to live a life, too."

"I hired Ms. Holcomb to help you, not to be a mother to our child."

"Then why don't you stay and help, or are you so busy helping other women that you knocked up! You think I don't know. I'm here suffering, and you're sticking your dick in all these gaping holes. What about me? I am your wife!"

"Ms. Holcomb!" Josea called.

"Yes," Ms. Holcomb said, rushing into the bedroom.

"You're fired," Josea said.

"No, she's not! Ms. Holcomb, you are staying," I demanded.

"What did I say?"

Josea rushed towards me, and I pulled the gun out and aimed it straight at him.

"I must learn to protect myself," I said.

Josea stood still with his hands up.

"If you think about hitting me, I will blow your damn brains out."

Poor Ms. Holcomb was scared and begged me not to do such a thing.

I figured it wasn't fair for my family to lose their freedom protecting me, and I was too much of a coward to defend myself.

"Jasmine will be with Ms. Holcomb for a few days while I get together. Do I make myself clear?" I asked.

I felt a sense of power that overtook me.

"Fine," Josea said.

I checked into a psychiatric ward to battle with suicidal ideations. I never attempted to end my life, but the temptations were getting too intense to bear. The nightmares and the constant voices raging inside of my mind left me hopeless.

Just end it, end it.

"NO!" I screamed and punched the wall.

Praying? Forget about it. I thought I was too far from God.

Once I was admitted, I could barely keep anything I had packed in my bag. I was living off the bare minimum. I sat on the hard bed and looked at my tennis shoes with no strings. I wondered how the hell I got here. I questioned who I was and whether I would ever be able to become half the woman my mama was. I knew Mama was rolling in her grave and was very displeased about my life. Everything she taught me seemed to be in vain.

After what seemed to be hours later, Dr. Fitz, a tall, thin white woman, arrived. She adjusted her glasses and asked me a bunch of questions about my mental health.

I was uncomfortable, but I knew this stage of my life was necessary so I could raise my daughter. I answered each question honestly. I was desperate to get help from anyone.

I was in a secured unit, locked in with a few other people, watching television or taking a short nap until a therapist arrived.

The only thing I looked forward to was the phone calls I had in the morning and before bedtime. Ms. Holcomb would hold the phone to Jasmine's ear and let me hear her babble.

"Mama is doing this for you," I said, smiling.

I was assigned a therapist, Ms. Gaston, an older white lady. I didn't like her and found it hard to open up. I gave her a difficult time. She tried so hard to pry into my life with her questions. I wasn't pleased with her fake smiles and forced laughter because nothing I said was amusing.

She was there to get paid, I was there to become a fit mother. Since she wanted to know what I was thinking, I asked her, "What did you think about the Civil Rights Movement?"

Ms. Gatson uncrossed her legs and eased up a bit.

Besides saying yes or no, that was the most I ever talked to her.

"I believe it was a wonderful thing. May I ask why you are concerned about my feelings toward the Civil Rights Movement?"

"Because segregation ended not too long ago, and I find it funny that nothing but a bunch of white people are here to help me," I said. "How am I supposed to know I'm no more than a social experiment? If my people had been allowed to get the same education, then maybe they would have been able to help me. Maybe they would understand how it feels to be raised in a Black church, so tied down to religion, to the point that making mistakes makes you feel like you don't belong in the world. Understanding that God doesn't move the same in everybody and when something bad happens, you call on God for help, not some so-called educated white woman, but you call on God. Not because you want to, but because you're Black, and that's the only thing you must do. God is the answer to everything. Did you know that? Of course, you don't."

"No offense, Ms. Gatson, but you remind me of a lady who was a racist bitch to my mama one day while we were out shopping. I wanted to badly punch her in her damn lips, but Mama told me that was not a nice thing to do because it wasn't *Godly*. I thought I would surely be strong in God like Mama, but that's not my story."

"I'm sorry that she made you feel that way," Ms. Gatson said. "I know that people's past—

"Black people's past," I interrupted. "Listen, Ms. Gaston, you can do nothing for me because I refuse to tell you any of my business. I am angry and depressed. Tell the doctor to prescribe me some medication so that I can get the hell out of here to see my daughter."

Ms. Gatson closed her notebook and stood up. "It was a pleasure meeting you."

I was released from the psych ward with my prescription, Tetracyclic. I called a taxi and headed home, anxiously waiting to see Jasmine and hold her after the longest week.

When I arrived, what I saw completely turned my world upside down and I dropped into the gates of Hell. My home was raided and surrounded by countless FBIs with guns, toting everything out of the house.

I exited the car, yelling, "What's going on?" *"Where is my baby?"*

I saw Josea arrested and screamed, "Josea, what happened? Where is our daughter?"

The policeman held me back, so I never got close to my husband.

Josea yelled, " Fue esa perra, la Sra. Holcomb, la que nos delató. Esa perra es una rata y ahora se llevaron a nuestro bebé!!!"

He said, "That it was that bitch, Ms. Holcomb. She told on us. That bitch is a rat and now they took our baby."

I was in shambles. I felt no good and defeated, so I wept on my knees. Ms. Holcomb betrayed us, and it was her idea that I go get help while she watched the baby. She wanted Jasmine for herself. She, too, was a wolf in sheep's clothing.

I thought I was never going to see Jasmine again.

"The judge granted me five years of probation," Ms. Maple cried. "It seemed like Jasmine was in and out of my life ever since. I don't know if she would ever forgive me."

"I'm sure there is still hope," Ivy said, consoling Ms. Maple.

"Eso espero," Ms. Maple said

"Yeah, I hope so, too," Ivy said, hugging Ms. Maple.

TWENTY-SEVEN

It was a slow Tuesday afternoon at Fancy Boutique Shop. Ivy spent most of her time thumbing through a magazine and chatting with Tally, who was in a pretty good mood.

Every now and then, Ivy greeted a customer. "Welcome to Fancy Boutique. Let me know if I can help you find anything," Ivy said.

"So, you're becoming an expert, I see," Tally said, smiling. She noticed Ivy wasn't shy speaking with customers and improved her sales. "You would be a manager in no time," Tally said.

"Well, I'm learning from the best," Ivy said, closing the magazine. "So, you're counting down the days for the ball."

"I am. Even though I am going by myself," Tally said, "I moved on, and I want to thank you, Ivy. I never thought you would become the friend that I needed."

"Same to you, Tally."

Ivy's relationship with Brian had become void. With the help of Ms. Honey and Ms. Maple, she slowly started to forgive herself for her decisions.

"So, it is not too late for you to go," Tally hinted, picking up a dress and pressing it against Ivy.

"So, you want me to look a mess when your dress is to die for?" Ivy said, laughing. "Ms. Maple is going to make you look so gorgeous."

"Oh, my god," Tally said, turning her head.

"Girl, what's wrong with you," Ivy asked.

"My cousin, Jasmine, just walked in here, and every time she sees family, she spazzes out like we all did something to her. The last thing I need is a commotion at work. Let me know when she's gone."

"Welcome to Fancy Boutique Shop," Ivy said, perking up a bit after the work day had dragged.

Jasmine barely acknowledged the friendly greeting as she shopped with her dark shades on. She continued to browse around the store, picking up a t-shirt off the rail and hanging it back.

"I think that would look good on you," Ivy said, trying to ease a conversation.

"Too bad I ain't spending forty dollars on a damn t-shirt," Jasmine said, and she continued to scan the boutique.

"Well, let me know if I can help you with anything," Ivy said, smiling.

"A piece of mind would be nice, so go ahead and leave me alone," Jasmine said, smirking.

Jasmine's mean gesture still left Ivy wondering how to start a conversation with her. Ivy stood behind the counter and tapped her fingers on the desk.

She thought that if I could get into Jasmine's good graces and reunite her with her mother, her purpose would be completed.

Ivy could not help but think about Ms. Maple's story and how much of a heartache it was. Ivy watched Jasmine from afar as she continued to browse the store, picking up items. Jasmine placed a T-shirt in her purse.

"I'm ready to check out now," Jasmine said, approaching the register with a small bottle of lotion.

"Will this be all for you?" Ivy said.

"Isn't this all you see," Jasmine said.

"You're right. I can't see the shirt you placed in your bag, Jasmine," Ivy said.

Jasmine snatched the shirt from her purse and dumped it on the counter.

"How in the hell do you know me?" Jasmine asked. "I Iuh?"

Ivy cringed, realizing that she put herself in an awkward position.

Jasmine cared nothing about the attempted theft charge and tried to control her temper before she snatched Ivy over the counter.

"Who are you, and how do you know me?" Jasmine asked, folding her arms and cocking her neck.

"I know your mother," Ivy said.

"Anita Holcomb is dead."

"No, I'm talking about your biological mother, Anna."

"You have no idea how much I despise that woman. I bet you don't know about what she put me through."

"I know that she is regretful, and I know that she loves you. Please, Jasmine–

"Who the hell are you?"

"My name is Ivy. I am a neighbor of your mother."

"My what?"

"Anna. I got to know Anna. Anna is so remorseful for what happened. I know forgiving people isn't the easiest thing to do, but I need you to hear me out about how much she loves and needs you in her life."

Jasmine lifted her shades and wiped the tears from her eyes.

"I didn't mean to make you cry," Ivy said.

"Well, that's too damn late," Jasmine said. She changed her tone and spoke through her sniffles. "I know she loves me, but I want her to experience the same pain she gave me all of those years growing up without her."

"I understand."

"Thanks for not calling the police. I don't need to spend another night in jail."

"No problem. In fact, I'll buy the lotion and shirt if you promise to go out to lunch with me," Ivy said, smiling. Deep inside, she knew she had gone too far, but she would do anything to make Ms. Maple happy.

The kind act was worth the risk, but Ivy knew she may have taken on more than she could handle. Ms. Maple and her daughter's relationship has been rocky for years.

"Sure," Jasmine said.

"You promise."

"I promise."

TWENTY- EIGHT

Life had been looking much better for Ivy. She was promoted to assistant manager at the boutique. To celebrate, Ms. Honey fixed a nice dinner and invited Maple over to celebrate Ivy's accomplishment.

This dinner was more than just a celebration of her job promotion. It was a celebration of a newfound life that she was stepping into.

A couple of months ago, Ivy was a complete mess and believed there was no hope for her. Now, she felt like she could accomplish anything, thanks to the help of newfound friends, whom she considered her mothers and her guardian angels, Maple and Honey.

That weekend was full of laughter, love, and light. Maple and Honey took the time to live in the present and appreciated the company Ivy kept them.

"Cheers to a new beginning," Maple said, raising her wine glass. "Ivy, we are very proud of you."

"Very proud is an understatement," Honey said as they clung their glasses in the air.

"Thanks for accepting me as if I were a daughter," Ivy said, holding back tears.

Ivy never told Maple she saw Jasmine and that she had met with her for lunch at her job. The conversation Ivy had with Jasmine was rough but hopeful. Ivy did not want Maple to feel like it was promising that they would reunite. Jasmine was stubborn and harbored a lot of hate in her heart.

Jasmine sat with Ivy for lunch every Tuesday.

"Life is so full of surprises if we just hold on," Honey said, taking up her empty dish. "Anybody need more wine?" she asked.

"Of course, Honey," Maple said.

"So, when will we get to the part of the story I am waiting on?" Ivy asked.

"What part?" Maple asked.

"When will you two meet?" Ivy asked anxiously as she sipped her wine.

"I think now would be the perfect time," Honey said, taking her seat and sipping her wine.

"I think I need to tell this one," Maple said, sipping her wine. "No offense, Honey, but my story about how we met is way more interesting."

Honey laughed and said, "Go ahead, girl."

"I worked hard as hell to get back on my feet so that I could be reunited with my daughter. Since I was on probation, I had to get a job, so I started working as an office clerk at a local warehouse. I'll never forget Mr. Grant, the boss, calling me into his office on a Friday afternoon."

IN 1988—

"Clara," Mr. Grant called. "I need to see you."

I stepped into his office and sat in front of his desk. I knew it was going to be some bullshit, but I had to accept whatever came out of his big mouth.

He sat down in his big, comfy chair like he was so important. I never saw Mr. Grant do any work besides throwing his authority around to other niggas in the building. I worked faithfully for almost two years as I saw him get fat from greed, over-eating from his underpaid employees' sweat and sacrifices.

He adjusted his gray tie and said, "Clara, I'm sorry, but I must let you go."

I felt anger rising in my chest, but I kept my composure. Along with getting a job, I had to take anger management as a condition for my probation. The anger management classes barely worked as I damn near cussed someone out every day. I took a few deep breaths and counted to five.

"Why?" I asked, looking at him to show that I cared about losing my job.

"Clara, you have been late many times."

"I had to meet with my probation officer, sir," I said.

"Not every day."

"I have to wait on the bus. I told you before I took that job that I had no means of transportation. I can't help the broken transportation system."

"I know, but your probation officer calls and comes in here looking for you, and it's just not a good look for the company," Mr. Grant said.

"You knew I was on probation when he hired me," I said, getting mad as hell. My foot was shaking. "You know I need this job."

I knew if I knocked his ass out, my actions would have sent me to jail. I would've gone ten steps backward to convince the court that I was a fit mother.

Mr. Grant wasn't worth the chance.

"You do know what I am up against," I said. I had never pleaded with a man before, but I was willing to swallow my pride for the sake of my future.

Mr. Grant uncovered his fake sympathy for me and nearly screamed, "Clara, you are terminated!"

"Watch your tone when you speak to me," I said sternly. "You give a nigga a little authority, and they act like they lost their got damn mind."

"Expect your last check next week," Mr. Grant said, pounding a stack of paper on his desk.

"Until we learn to treat each other better, we will never progress," I said. "Black motherfucker!"

"Well, well, well. You and the Jim Crow Laws have something in common. You're both gone."

"Too bad Uncle Tom is still around. Now, kiss my ass!" I said, slamming the door on my way out.

I left the building and wondered how to explain this to my probation officer. I thought I would never have my daughter in my custody again.

I went home and knew that crying wouldn't solve anything, but it helped relieve my frustration of facing another setback. So, I took off my office clothes and took a long, hot shower, leaning my head against the wall and letting the water pound against my face.

I tried being a good woman, the model citizen who did the right things, only to get screwed by a man whose skin completion matched mine.

Later that night, I put away those thrift store office clothes and pulled the skimpiest black skirt and shirt out of my closet. I was now, again, *Maple*.

When I returned to the streets, it was like I never left. I felt the excitement and the burst of high that would cover my pain temporarily. I was delusional to think that I was in control of my fate, but that's what addiction did for me. Besides, I had to make a living somehow.

The only thing that was hard for me to accept was that I was older and I was a mother. I stood on the corner with some younger girls who had a pimp telling them what to do. I saw how frightened they were and said it would never be me.

I met one guy who was actually nice-looking. He was handsome. He forgot to take off his wedding ring, so I asked, "What is a married man doing out here, buying sex from a stranger?"

He hung his head down in shame.

Usually, I wouldn't give a damn, but that night I did. I cared about his wife, who had no idea he was sneaking around.

"Why is a beautiful woman out here selling her body?" he asked me.

Like him, I hung my head down in shame.

"That's fair enough," I said, sitting on the passenger side of his car.

"We don't have to do this," he said.

"Thank you," I told him.

I left, and he told me to be careful. That was the first time I turned down an opportunity to make any money. I was changing, and I had to accept my fate: This life would end me in a deep hole, a hole six feet under, if I kept going.

I went home, furious. I had yet to learn how to land another job. Who would want to hire me? I had nobody to turn to, so I called Clarissa.

Clarissa cursed me out and said she was no longer a part of my family.

This is it, I thought. *This is where I end my life.* But first, I had an urge to visit my mama's grave, so I would head to the bus station the first chance I had.

I remember telling her as a child, "How do you know people are in Heaven? How do you know people are not just sleeping in their graves?" Either answer, it was better than being alive.

I caught a cab that evening with one suitcase that carried a loaded gun. I had a plan. I would cry my eyes out over Mama's grave and then end my life there.

"I need one bus ticket to Tuskegee, Alabama," I said.

I had just enough money, but the bus wouldn't leave until the next morning around 5:15. I checked my watch, and it was only 11:30 that night. I sat on the cold, hard seat and waited. That was how I imagined my body. Cold and hard.

People were there, but I saw no one, if that made sense. Clouds of judgment filled my mind. I contemplated my love and my death speech to my mama. At the time, I knew Jasmine would be better without me.

Time was running slow, and I had no sleep before making a random decision to leave my home to head thousands of miles away. I was outside waiting for the bus until I fell asleep on one of the benches and nearly missed my boarding time.

"Hey, there–where do you think your fine ass is going?"

I woke up to the voice of a guy who, at one time, paid me for sexual favors. He called himself a pimp now and had women working underneath him.

I never knew his name. I only knew he wouldn't last too long because he was a loud, arrogant bastard.

"You know if you work for me–

"Save it! I don't work for nobody, so take your ass somewhere else. I ain't no weak woman. I work for myself. You got that?"

He threw his hands up and backed away. "Hey, I was just offering."

Then, I heard a woman's voice that was opposite his.

"I like the way you handle yourself."

"Who are you?" I asked.

"My name is Honey. Do you want a cigarette? Or maybe you are one of those bougie girls," Honey said, taking a pack of cigarettes from her purse.

Honey had just returned to town from attending her sister's graduation in Chicago.

"I ain't never seen a bougie girl sleeping at a bus station," I said, picking out a cigarette from the pack and holding it out for her to light it. "My name is Maple."

"Maple? I heard your name ringing in the streets a couple of times."

"I'm sure you have. Why are you at the bus station this early?" I asked, noting that it was near 4:15 A.M.

"The damn bus never runs on time. My older sister graduated from nursing school. She's on her way to becoming an OBGYN," Honey said, "I'm proud of her."

"So, she's a doctor, and you're a whore."

"A damn good one."

I liked that answer. It was some shit that I would have said when someone tried to insult me too.

"Well, I'm giving up that life," I said. "I'm headed out, and I ain't coming back. It ain't nothing here for me. Not a damn thing."

"Not even one," Honey said. "Life is crazy, especially when you're doing it alone."

"I do have a daughter. It's a long story, but—

"You ain't gotta tell me shit. I know life blows hard."

"Every waking moment of my life hurts like hell. A sting in my heart must go one way or the other. I can't fight anymore." I blew the smoke out of my lungs into the cold air.

Honey eased her way onto the bench, sitting next to me. There was something about her presence that assured me that I wasn't supposed to take that ride to Alabama and end my life.

"Anything worth having is worth fighting for," Honey said, blowing smoke from her lungs.

"What are you fighting for?"

Honey took a while to answer.

"I want to make my mama proud even though she's dead. I don't want her teachings to be in vain."

In an instant, I knew Honey and I had something deeply in common. Besides the street life, we had to find our purpose. I looked out and saw the bus for me to travel on arrived. I looked at my bus ticket and ripped it.

"Seemed like you changed your mind," Honey said.

Tears streaming down my eyes, "I want my daughter back."

"Maple, I think we would be stronger together."

"Let me make this clear. I'm only staying around to be reunited with my daughter. This is business. I ain't looking for a best friend."

"That's a deal," Honey said.

Honey invited Maple to stay with her until she was stable enough to maintain herself. They got acquainted with one another effortlessly. Before they knew it, they found out that they shared so much in common. Honestly, it was scary how soon they latched on to each other's hearts and became close as sisters, even though they had slight, noticeable differences in personalities.

Honey kept her room neat and tidy. Maple's room was a little messy, tossing her clothes everywhere. Honey thought it was because Maple's mind was everywhere too. But one thing for sure, they kept a picture of the family close by their beds. Maple and Honey would tell stories about their family, then cry and laugh at the same story.

Ironically, Honey landed her a job at a local library. It was a job Honey had never imagined working at since she had never done well in school. Moving those books around constantly reminded her about her failure to succeed in school. Ms. Shirley, her boss, needed someone to sort the new and rented books alphabetically. It took Honey some time to get used to working a nine-to-five, but she felt a little better about herself. Honey knew that she was making an honest wage. At 32, Honey knew that the hustle and bustle of staying out all night was not the answer to the change she desperately needed. The change was challenging, but she pushed through.

Maple worked as a clerk at a gas station and hoped to one day have custody of her daughter, Jasmine. She worked earnestly and occasionally checked in with her case manager, Ms. Hail, to check on her progress. About once a month, Maple visited her daughter, who has bounced around in different foster homes. Each time she saw Jasmine, a rush of emotions overwhelmed her. Maple would get anxious again, and the feeling of guilt overwhelmed her. Maple never knew what mood Jasmine would be in. Sometimes, Jasmine would be happy; other times, she would barely respond or look her way. It had been years, and Jasmine became numb to the recurring line, "You will be with me one day, I promise."

"How was the visit?" Honey asked Maple, who came inside the home, took off her coat, and hung it up. Maple breathed a sigh of relief.

"It wasn't too bad today," Maple said. "She at least shook her head when I told her that I loved her." Maple considered the last time Jasmine screamed and refused to enter the room to meet her. It took the case manager a while to convince Jasmine she was safe.

Honey could always find it challenging to talk to Maple about Jasmine. Honey didn't want to cause any unwanted triggers.

"Ms. Hail told me that I should be getting her back soon, but of course, the judge always seems to find fault in me. They just want my Black baby in the system. Every time I go into the courtroom, they want to bring up my got-damn past. How can I get over something when they keep making me feel like a fuck-up?"

"Don't allow them to get to you too badly. I can only imagine how hard it is. Maybe next time, I can go with you."

"Honey, you got to work."

"I will take off."

Maple smiled faintly. She never imagined a woman she met at a bus station, wearing a long trench tan coat, would be her sister's keeper.

Honey indeed took a load off of Maple.

"I figured we need to go out," Honey said. "We both have been working our asses off, and we need to have a little fun."

Maple was skeptical. She remembered the last time she went out and had a little fun. It turned out to be a complete nightmare—a night that scorned her for the rest of her life, leaving her without a family or a shoulder to lean on. It was like a domino effect of losses.

"C'mon girl, a little light dinner, nothing crazy," Honey said, considering that her friend had to be careful. "Besides, we're getting too damn old to be messing around all night."

"You do be tucked away and in your bed like a grandmother," Maple said, joking.

Honey laughed, but the truth was Honey wasn't always sleeping. Working at the library awoke a dream that she had never shared with anyone. Honey dreamed of being an author due to having a vivid imagination. But knowing she could barely read or spell correctly made her feel foolish. So, she tucked herself away and wrote in secret, afraid to be judged. Feeling afraid to be laughed at.

Honey checked her watch and said, "We should be getting ready soon. Dinner is on me."

Honey and Maple had the time of their lives. Talking shit, laughing at people, and eating good soul food. After a rough day, Honey knew what her best friend needed.

When they were together, the only feeling they had could only be described as 'fuck everything.' The hell with always being worried about situations that they no longer controlled.

Time slipped by, and the restaurant was nearly closed before Honey paid the bill, and they left, holding and swinging each other's hands. Honey forgot that she was not much of a drinker. Two glasses of wine had her giddy.

"Hey, you two mamas," a voice called out. The young man was wearing a big gold chain around his neck.

They saw his chain before they noticed his multicolored neon bucket hat, wearing an oversized blue tracksuit. He had a stack of invitations in his hands.

"Allow me to properly introduce myself. My name is Pierre Leflare, and I swear I'm the finest in town!"

Maple and Honey couldn't hold their laughter at the young man approaching them on the street.

"Boy, how old are you?" Maple asked as she continued to laugh in his face.

"I'm twenty-three. What about you, Old Mamas?"

"Old! little boy, go find somebody else to play with. You still got milk behind the ears," Maple said, laughing.

"I bet he still remembers what his mama's nipples taste like," Honey said.

"Hey, you two can joke all you want. But, I'm the man you both will need," Pierre said, not allowing them to steal away his confidence.

"What do you have there?" Honey asked, snatching the invitations out of his hand.

"I am a bar owner. Freshly new in town. It's called the Motown Paradise. We got good music, and we got good food. I saw two fine ol—*mature* women, and I said, hey, I need them to come to work with me as my waitresses. I know I look like a skinny little kid, but I'm making big money moves in the city. I just think you two should come and check it out next Friday night," Pierre said, smiling.

"I don't do the club thang," Maple said. "Too much trouble, and you little, young niggas don't know how to act." She took the invitations out of Honey's hand and returned them to Pierre, who showed his disappointment.

"The extra money could help," Honey whispered, nudging Maple's shoulder.

Maple believed that the cheap wine was talking, not Honey's right mind.

"Honey   really?"

"I'm just saying. Things are getting a little tight, and the money is legal. We will give it a try," Honey said, taking the card back from Pierre. "And if we see an ounce of trouble, we will walk out anytime. Do you hear me?" Honey asked sternly.

Pierre's face lit like gold. He thought Maple and Honey were the perfect women to work at Motown Paradise because of their strong presence.

Pierre said, "Oh, sweet! So, what may I call you beautiful, young-looking women?"

"I'm Honey, and this is Maple."

"You see, I was with you all the way until you told that lie," Honey said, looking at Maple.

"What lie did I tell?"

"You know you wanted to work in that club, not me. How dare you try to get Ivy to believe that I dragged you into working there?" Honey asked, laughing. She recalled telling her friend that being around a potentially raunchy crowd wasn't the best idea. Around that time, the city was infested with Cocaine.

Ivy shook her head and thought it was strange that Ms. Honey would push Ms. Maple to work at a nightclub after all she had been through.

"Well, that's how I remembered it. Besides, you were too drunk to know," Maple laughed.

Before they knew it, they found themselves sitting around the table until midnight, catching up on the latest gossip in the city.

"I guess I better get going," Maple said, putting on her coat to take a brisk walk home.

"We will watch you out the door," Honey said. "And let me tell the story next time, please."

TWENTY-NINE

The next day, Honey was in solitude, looking out the window and drinking her morning coffee. She got a late start but was in no rush to do anything but reflect on how far she had come. For the first time in a while, Honey felt boastful yet humbled that it wasn't her own will that she made it through treacherous moments. She no longer had imposter syndrome, and her life wasn't anything short of extraordinary. She touched her heart to calm down the surreal feelings that she made it over...*Every. Single. Damn. Thing.*

She sipped her coffee. The hurtful parts of telling her story were almost over, and it would trample into what she called a burst of colorful fireworks. Out of all the women she met, she was in awe that Ivy encouraged her to be brave enough to bare it all and show that her story mattered too, even the ugly secrets.

"Good morning," Ivy said,

Honey turned her head and was pleasantly surprised that she saw Ivy.

"I thought you were at work," Honey said, smiling. "I'll make you a fresh cup of coffee if you would like."

"I am off today," Ivy said, seeing that the coffee was just fine the way it was. She poured herself a cup and joined Honey at the kitchen table. She noticed Honey appeared to be refreshed. "I had such a great time last night with you and Ms. Maple," Ivy said.

Last night, Ivy's stomach was aching from all of the laughter.

"Maple is a mess."

Ivy sipped her coffee and waited for Honey to continue the story. Honey began to tell her truth...

Maple and I started working at Motown Paradise, leaving our regular nine-to-five. On Friday and Saturday nights, we had the biggest crowd and received better tips from our customers. We cursed, drank, and danced with the people to keep them entertained. But something was missing in both of us. Maple and I still knew we were misguided women who kept busy to avoid our past memories. We fell in and out of love with boyfriends and spent most of our time looking for love, only to find our hearts broken and minds blackout from over-drinking. It was a circle of mess. Before we knew it, time had passed, and we found ourselves wasting time with no real purpose. Maple and I would sit around our dining room for many days and discuss what we wanted to be before we realized we were still making fast money and weren't getting any younger.

People would ask Maple.

"So, why do they call you Maple?"

Maple would say, "Because I am sweet, but too much of me isn't good for you."

And that was nothing but the truth. It was an honest answer for both of us, so I started using that line, too.

One night, I was sitting at the kitchen table, minding my business, when Maple came in and joined me. I don't know what made me ask her this, but the question slipped out.

"Maple, do you believe in God?"

Maple, who was somewhat hungover, holding a glass of water, looked at me curiously. We never spoke about our beliefs or religion.

"I want to," Maple said. "My mama told me that you have to be hot or cold. If you are lukewarm, then God will spit you out. If there's a God, I'd rather stay hot and keep out of God's mouth. Certainly, I want to pray, but how could He hear me when I have done so much wrong?"

Maple leaned back and folded her arms. "What about you?"

"I really want to believe in Him, but I don't know, Maple. I just don't know," I said slowly, wondering if I was even worthy of mentioning His name.

There was a long moment of silence before we parted ways. I went into my room and collapsed on my knees in front of my mama's picture. For the first time in a long time, I prayed quietly, tears streaming from my eyes.

I can't quite remember what I said, but I would give God a chance to show me He existed.

I remember it was a Friday night when Maple and I were working at Motown Paradise when God answered the prayer we didn't know we needed. We met an old woman named Sugar. And Sugar—well, she awakened the dream we had suppressed for a long time.

I was behind the bar talking with Pierre, who ran around it like a chicken with its head cut off, sweating. He always found himself busy making sure the music was right, the drinks were flowing, and the food was good. Pierre was hardworking and mature for his age. He took great pride in his work.

"How's everything going, Honey?" he asked for the tenth time that night. He would check on his staff like clockwork to make sure that we didn't have any complaints or be harassed by any customers.

"You know how it's going," I said. I was burnt out, and my feet were aching. I thought to myself, *I am tired of this shit.* But I was thankful.

I looked at the entrance and noticed an older lady casually walking inside the club. She was stunning in her black leather coat and hat, and her dark, curly gray hair stuck out underneath it.

"Granny, what are you doing here?" Pierre said, stopping in his tracks. Finally, he slowed down and set drinks on the counter. "Honey, please serve these drinks to Table Five," he said, looking embarrassed.

"Don't you, Granny, me," Sugar said, lifting her petite frame on the stool in front of the bar. "So, this is what you spent your grandfather's inheritance on? A club full of booty-shaking heathens!"

Half of the clubbers were drunk or high off of cocaine, dancing to the beat of 80's Hip Hop in their shell-toe sneakers.

"Granny, this is not a place for you."

"Don't tell me where I can't go. I told my son not to give you money until you are mature enough to handle it. Spending hardworking money that your grandfather worked all his life for on booze and sinners."

"Granny, how did you get here?"

"I caught a cab. What kind of service is this? I want a coke."

"Granny-

Sugar grabbed him by his collar and yanked him over the bar. "Boy, give me a coke!"

Pierre quickly grabbed a glass and poured a cold Coke for his granny. Then, he handed it over and wished she would leave so they could discuss it later. Sugar glanced around and made herself comfortable, watching people shaking their asses and doing the latest dances to Hip-Hop music between Milli Vanilli, The Ed Lover Dance, and the Cabbage Patch, to name a few.

"You could at least play some music that makes sense. What is this gibberish?"

"Granny, this isn't the 40s. This is the 80s, which means you don't need to be here," Pierre said, grinning uncomfortably. He was embarrassed that his 93-year-old granny was sitting in a nightclub with a bunch of youngsters.

"Boy, if it wasn't for your grandaddy touching me, you wouldn't be here. I'm grown," she said, drinking her Coke. "This Coke is FLAT!"

"Well, you don't drink anything else."

"Give me some water and light on the ice."

"No problem."

"And get rid of that flat Coke!"

He hurried and gave her what she wanted so she could leave. However, Sugar stayed and watched.

"Hey, you," Sugar said, looking at me. She smiled. I wanted to cover up my legs and pull down my shirt to cover myself. I felt like a bashful little girl who had no business leaving the house.

"Hey," I said. "How can I help you?"

Sugar looked me up and down, then cocked her head to the side. She smiled, clapped her hands, and then placed her small right hand on her hips.

"Are you related to a woman named Dessie?"

No matter who someone was, if they knew Dessie, they knew I was her daughter. There was no denying that I was a spitting image of Mama. I smiled a little and was afraid of what she might say.

"That was my mama."

"Lord, have mercy. Your mama used to work for me. I'm Mrs. Johnston, but some call me Sugar. Your mother was the sweetest woman I ever met."

"Who's the old lady?" Maple whispered in my ear, but she kept moving before I could answer.

I walked towards Ms. Sugar and said, "It's nice to finally meet you."

Sugar damn near cried when I held her hand. She told me that she was sorry that she was unable to attend my mama's funeral and that she was near death herself at the time. She thought that she would've been sleeping in her grave, too.

The music was loud, so she wasted no time getting to her point.

"I want you to come by my place on Sunday evening. I feel like I owe you a part of my heart. Bring your friend with you," she said, giving me her address. She left me no room to say no thank you.

It was Karaoke night, and Sugar took the stage. Pierre's face turned red as he watched Sugar holding the mic. She was no more than 5'2 and no more than 120 in weight, but she had the rowdy crowd's attention when she tapped the microphone.

"What is she about to do?" Pierre asked himself as he hung his head down.

I knew Pierre wanted to snatch the mic from her and escort her out of the building, but he was too respectful, and there was no telling how Sugar would've snatched him up again.

Sugar had everyone's attention. She held that mic up to her pink lips and sang boldly. *Jesus loves me—ohhhhh—-Jesus loves me...Jesus loves you——oooooo, Jesus loves you.*

I turned my face to the left of me and saw Maple weeping a little. I asked if she was okay.

Maple said, "I haven't heard the Gospel in a long time."

When Sugar was finished singing, she was shown love from the crowd.

Pierre helped his granny off the stage, lending her a hand so she wouldn't trample down the few steps.

"Thanks, granny," Pierre said.

"No problem. I wish I had a COKE!"

Sunday evening came, and I convinced Maple to join me in meeting Ms. Sugar at her home. Her real name was Susie, but people started calling her Sugar. We arrived at the two-brick-story home with the perfect, manicured green grass. As we stood on the porch, decorated with outside furniture, we knew Sugar had money.

I knocked on the door and waited, looking around.

A minute later, Ms. Sugar opened the door and greeted us with a warm, loving smile.

"Hey, ladies, come on in," she hugged us individually. "Come in and take a seat."

I couldn't help but think that this was the place my mama used to clean up. I imagined her wearing her blue uniform, strolling throughout the house, making the home spotless. I was overwhelmed that my mama spent some of her last days on Earth here. Before I knew it, Maple was in front of me, and I took my time to finally see where my mama's last job was.

"Are you okay?" Maple asked. Maple repeatedly told me that I did not have to come if it would make me uncomfortable, but I insisted that I had to know what Ms. Sugar wanted with us. I felt Ms. Sugar ought to be ashamed that my family had to scrape for pennies to bury my mama, and not one cent was given on behalf of Sugar's family. But my mama only spoke sweet words about Ms. Sugar.

"I'm fine," I said, joining them in the living room, where we had cups of tea on the coffee table.

"Help yourselves," Ms. Sugar said.

"Thanks for welcoming us into your home," Maple said. She made small talk because she knew I was having mixed feelings.

It was like Ms. Sugar read my mind.

"Clara, your mother was an angel of mine. She took good care of my home and kept me in great company. Sometimes, she'd come here to talk and laugh with me all night. We'd sit at the table, right over there, chatting away. She spoke so well of you and your sister. It felt like I knew you already," she said. "You see this nice house, but I don't own anything. As soon as my husband died, my oldest found a way to get power of attorney over me. I tell you, I'm too old to let anyone send me to Hell, including my own children. We can't take anything with us when we are good and gone."

"Isn't that the truth," Maple said.

Ms. Sugar was a wise woman who talked a lot. Her roots were embedded in South Carolina, and she became a school teacher before she married the love of her life, William, who became a surgeon. She told us the entire spill of her life, but more importantly to us, she complimented us and treated us like we were queens. Before the day was gone, we found ourselves sitting in the dining area under a vast, shining chandelier. To our surprise, she had a chef who cooked a marvelous steak dinner served with red wine.

I had never eaten on fancy plates with nice silverware. A part of me felt out of place, somewhat undeserving of being treated so wonderfully. I waited until Ms. Sugar picked up her fork to eat her salad so I wouldn't start eating with the wrong utensil. Maple looked like she was in Heaven and didn't mind asking for more wine.

Besides being treated grandly, Ms. Sugar's wisdom was forever embedded in our minds as we listened intently to her regal voice. Not once did she bring up religion, but I knew she had God inside her from the first day we met at Motown Paradise.

"You two are so gorgeous," she said, "Looking like models. I remember when I was young, and well, at nineteen, I was married. Anyway, it's never too late to live your dreams," she said, taking small bites of her food.

Ms. Sugar checked her watch and said, "It's getting late. I will let Mr. Chad, my driver, take you two home."

Maple and I looked at each other, astonished that we were assisted inside a limousine to be headed to our home.

"See you next week," Ms. Sugar had said.

Every Sunday afternoon, we went to Ms. Sugar's house, getting more comfortable and allowing ourselves to be vulnerable a little. Strangely, I believed we were becoming little girls again, seeking answers from Mama. Ms. Sugar had a sense of humor and was very witty for her age. I saw why my mama didn't mind working for her. One day, she pulled me aside and handed me a check.

"I owe you this," she said, smiling. "Take it and do what you please."

That night, I called Erica and said with tears streaming down my eyes, "Erica, our prayer had been answered. We have enough money to buy our mama a tombstone."

"Yes, yes. God is good!" Erica said.

"Yes, He is!" I said, then I caught myself and realized what happened. I agree that *GOD IS GOOD*. I had spent years without praying and wondered if God was really present for me, and out of my excitement, I was hopeful. I knew to keep praying, and perhaps years of unanswered prayer requests would suddenly be answered.

A couple of days later, Erica flew from California, and we both were able to pick and purchase the perfect tombstone for our mama. We felt like a piece of our hearts was completed. I felt like the ropes tied tightly around my feet were being loosened, and a burden was being lifted.

"Mama, I sure hope you can rest more now," Erica said, hugging me.

I said nothing, just a sense of overwhelming peace took place inside of me. My hero, my mama, who sacrificed so much for everyone else to have something, finally had her resting spot completed.

DESSIE MARIE BROWN

Sunrise November 17, 1938- Sunset June 21, 1969

"As Sweet as Pie"

It was like we could not wait until Sunday evenings. Every time we went, it was like a revival. Her home was a place of healing.

"How about you two go to church with me?" Ms. Sugar asked, smiling wide.

Maple and I looked at each other and wondered if it would be okay. We have not stepped foot in a church in a long time and were hesitant.

At one point, Maple had said, "I can't imagine going to church without Mama by my side. I don't think I'm strong enough to do it."

To my surprise, Maple said, "Yes, we should go."

Ms. Sugar clapped her hands and did a little dance, then asked us to follow her to her room. There, she opened her closet, revealing a whole side of hat boxes.

"Ms. Sugar, you love hats like my mama did," Maple said, in awe of how many hats Ms. Sugar owned.

"Go ahead and try one on," Ms. Sugar said.

Maple opened one of the boxes and placed the white designer hat on her head in front of the mirror. I laughed a little because Maple looked like an old woman underneath that brim. A strong, Black church mother.

"This is the same hat my mama wanted," Maple said as a tear dripped down her smooth black skin.

I placed my hand on her shoulder to comfort her.

"I heard her voice," Maple said.

I asked, "What did she say?"

She said, "Only a woman with a dark hue and a head full of thick hair can give this style any justice."

After church, we sat at the dining room table the following Sunday. Ms. Sugar rambled on about how excited she was that we joined her in fellowship. She teased us and told us to watch out for Deacon So and So and Brother So and So because they were not good men.

"I saw them looking. They came over and spoke to me, but they didn't *ever* speak to me!" Ms. Sugar said, laughing. "They had their eyes wandering."

It was okay because we were not into churchmen, especially me.

"I'll be ninety-four next month and have nothing to wear." Ms. Sugar said. She had been talking about her birthday for the past two months.

"I'll make you a dress," Maple said.

"You design dresses?" Ms. Sugar asked, impressed.

"My mama taught me how to sew, and I started designing," Maple said. "It would be an honor to design you a nice gown for your birthday."

"I want a jazzy blue dress with a little razzle-dazzle. I know I'm old, but I want a nice split in the back. Can you do that?" Ms. Sugar asked, sipping her tea.

"I sure can," Maple said.

"Ms. Sugar loved her dress. In fact, it was the last fancy gown she wore," Honey said. "She gave Maple and me the strength we needed. She was our angel. She was the reason Maple and I began to see the light again."

"Such a beautiful story," Ivy said.

"Now, it is," Honey said, giggling.

Honey was proud to confront her past. It was like a healing journey that she did not know she needed.

"What about your love life?" Ivy asked. She was sure Honey had met a man she clinched to somewhere in her life. Although Honey never married, she had two sons she spoke to every day on the phone.

"Oooh, that Richard. I love him. He's still a sweet man," Honey said, "I got to head to the store. I'll tell you about him next time."

THIRTY

Ivy ordered lunch for two and sat at the table while she waited for Jasmine to arrive. She ordered a salmon salad and ordered Jasmine, her favorite, a BLT. Ivy was on lunch break, and she spent an hour every Tuesday meeting with Jasmine to chat and have heart-to-heart conversations about life.

Jasmine slowly opened up to her, even after she accused her of bribing her with food. But Ivy had every bit of intention to reunite Jasmine with her mother. Ivy believed Jasmine still loved Maple but was deeply misunderstood and confused about what love looks like. They had some things in common, but Ivy was always willing to be a listening ear.

Ivy checked her watch and saw it was approaching 12:30 P.M., and she was nervous Jasmine wouldn't show up. She sipped her lemonade and tasted her salad. If Jasmine did not show up in five minutes, she decided to box up her food and give it away.

"Hey," Jasmine said.

"I'm glad you decided to join me," Ivy said, smiling.

"I was nervous about coming," Jasmine said, taking a seat and sliding the BLT away from her. "I'm not hungry. Perhaps you can save it for later."

That was not like Jasmine to deny food. Ivy knew something was terribly wrong.

"What's going on?" Ivy asked. She lost her appetite and waited for Jasmine to answer. Jasmine looked around the restaurant before she grabbed her Sprite and took a long gulp with her trembling hand.

"I'm leaving the city...for good," Jasmine said. "Thank you for everything, but I don't want to be here anymore." Tears formed in her eyes.

Jasmine hurried off without any explanation other than feeling like she had enough. Ivy dropped money on the table and followed her outside the door.

"Jasmine...wait, please," Ivy begged, unsure if she would listen. "Why are you leaving? What about your mom?"

"She doesn't need to know," Jasmine said, turning around to face Ivy. "There's no reason for her or anybody to know where I will be."

"Jasmine-

"Listen, I know what you were trying to do, but it's not happening. That woman failed me, and I will never find the strength to forgive. I'll find another family. One thing I learned in my life is that when you get old, you can create your own life, and there's no reason to create a bond that was never there."

"Ms. Maple loves you. You are her only daughter. She has been through so much. Just sit and listen to her, and you will understand. I learned so much about your mom in the short time I've known her. And let me tell you, she is the most loving person I have ever met. She needs you as much as you need her. You don't want to hear this, but you two have much in common. Please don't do your mama like this. Please, don't do it to yourself. You deserve a mother's love, and it's not too late."

Ivy hoped she listened because she promised Ms. Honey that she would get Jasmine to be back with her Ms. Maple. Ivy would feel absolutely terrible, so she poured her heart out as if it was her last speech in the middle of a busy sidewalk.

Finally, Jasmine said, "Thanks for all you have done. Goodbye." She turned and hurried away, carrying that one bag on her shoulder that nearly tilted her over as she walked.

Ivy realized she bit off more than she could chew. Like Ms. Maple had said, Jasmine was stubborn and moody. But somehow, Ivy believed she would convince Jasmine to get her mom another chance. Ivy knew if something terrible happened to Jasmine, she would blame herself for failing a reunion. Ivy wiped away the joy she had imagined on Ms. Maple's face. Ivy sighed, knowing how important that day would have been.

Ivy was not productive at work and was glad the day was over with. She got to Ms. Honey's house, dropped on the soft bed, and flung her heels off. She rolled over, saw a black binder, and had no idea where it came from. She opened and read the title, *Where Hearts are Found*, written by Clara Brown. Intrigued, she began to turn the old pages one by one. She grabbed the binder and headed downstairs to meet Ms. Honey, who was watching TV in her living room.

"Ms. Honey," Ivy said, "you left your binder on the bed."

Ms. Honey turned the TV volume down and gave her full attention to Ivy.

"Oh, yes. I placed it there on purpose. I shared everything else with you. I figured I should go ahead and share my book," Honey said, smiling at the unpublished work. "I never had anyone read it, not even Maple. I would love to have your opinion on it."

"Why hasn't anyone read it?" Ivy asked.

"I'm too scared. I wasn't much of a speller and never finished school, so I was nervous about how others would think of me," she said. "I finished that book nearly forty years ago on an old big computer, probably made in the seventies," Honey said, laughing. "Paid a penny a page at a library. That's the only copy I have."

Ivy held the hundred and sixty-three-page binder like treasure. "Ms. Honey, I'd be glad to read your book."

"Are you going to keep it honest?"

"I will, and I have a little fact about myself. My minor was English in college," Ivy said. "And my mother's best friend is a publisher in New York," Ivy said, winking her left eye.

Honey tried not to get too excited. It would be a dream for her to finally publish her book and become an author. Who would've thought that she would have written a book? Instead of responding with pure excitement, Honey nodded her head.

"Yes, that would be nice."

THIRTY-ONE

Where Hearts Are Found was a book filled with romance and suspense. Ivy turned the pages and longed for more of this hidden masterpiece tucked in an old black binder. Honey outdid herself, writing about an old farmer named George, who planted seeds in a garden and stumbled across a diamond ring in the dirt with an engraved name. George, a single man who had never been married, found the woman, Barbara, who purposely buried the ring in hopes that her true love would find her. After going across town, George met her, and after a series of losses, they eloped.

Ivy finished the book within two days before she shook her head and thought about how shameful it would be to keep a story from the world. Honey's words evoked a light within her, and she knew *Where Hearts Are Found* would be a much-needed read for the masses who doubted love.

Ivy rushed down the stairs to tell Honey how much she adored the story.

"Did you really love it?" Honey asked, balling her dress into her hands. She was shocked that it only took Ivy the weekend to read her book.

"Yes, yes!" Ivy said. "It's...*magical!*"

"But, I know it is so far from perfect. I don't write that well."

"That's why I will be your editor," Ivy said. "I promise I will do everything possible to have your book published. You deserve to have your dreams come true."

Honey sat and said, "Being an author was a long dream of mine, but I never did well in school. I was just a wild woman with a crazy imagination. Ivy, I won't know how to thank you enough if this comes true."

"Ms. Honey, I got you."

Ivy took a seat next to her on the sofa.

"What inspired you to write this? This must have something to do with the love of your life, Richard," Ivy said, smiling.

"Oh, there's no love story like how I met Richard," Honey said. " Let me tell you."

IN 1991–

After Ms. Sugar died, I still went to church occasionally. It was something I ought to do to keep me from straying too far. I still had my imperfections and hot temperaments, especially with men.

Most of the time, I sat at the back of the church so I could slip out when I got tired of hearing Reverend Thompson huffing and puffing over the microphone or to avoid Richard, who somehow always found his way to greet me. I began to think that Jesus was an afterthought when he came to church because I was his number one. He smiled and waved at me, and I would wave and then turn my head, pretending that I wasn't studying him. Richard was fine and chiseled with a picture-perfect smile, showing pearly white teeth on his brownish skin. I wouldn't have minded learning more about him. But, other single women were attending the church too, and I saw how they followed him out the door and threw a little side leg at him or hugged him from the front so that he could feel their breasts.

Church whores. That's what I called them. They were nothing but plain old church whores who thought they were slick.

One Sunday, Richard caught up with me, and I had no choice but to talk to him because I did not want to come off rude, and I wanted to piss the rest of those ladies off. I meant *church whores.*

"Why are you always in such a hurry?" Richard asked, sounding all authoritative.

I thought this Negro got to be kidding me? He finally caught me and asked me boldly why I was in such a hurry. This Negro, who stood about four inches taller than me with my heels on, dared to sternly ask me about my business.

That shit turned me on. I leaned back a little and placed my hands on my hip.

"There's no need for me to stay around when God is done," I said, looking up into his slanted eyes.

He laughed. "So, what is your name?"

I thought, should I give him the street name or the name my mama gave me? The old me would have taken Richard for a joy ride, giving him the best pleasures of his life and had him falling in love, then leaving him in the dust with a broken heart. The best sex of his life, but a broken heart to mend, only to find that no other woman can do half the tricks I knew. But, lucky for him, I changed.

"Clara," I said, smiling. He had no idea how sweet and sticky Honey was.

"I'm Richard," he said. " It's nice to *finally* speak to you face to face."

I saw the church whores from the corner of my eye looking our way. Reverend Thompson just finished preaching how jealousy was as cruel as the grave. They were killing me with their eyes.

I started giggling for the hell of it. "Would you be kind enough to walk me to my car?" I asked.

"Sure."

We took a little stroll across the street and onto the parking lot to stop by my black truck.

"Clara, I would like to take you out Friday night and get to know you as a friend. You're beautiful," Richard said, opening the car door.

"Sure, Richard."

Richard and I have become inseparable ever since. We could not stay away from each other. He would leave working from the factory to shower, then come over and keep me company for hours. On his off days, we would explore new food or stay in and play cards, laughing and joking around with Maple.

For the first time, I was falling in love and not in lust. A few months flew by, and we had not been intimate yet. I never felt pressured to have sex with him, or he was actually a Christian man who was devoted to keeping clean. I saw no fault in him. I felt like I did not deserve Richard in my space. To me, he was perfect, and I still had a residue of shame left on me, and no matter how hard I wiped, the stain of guilt was still there to keep me from exposing my whole heart.

Richard was funny without trying to be. Every now and then, Richard would slip and say, *shit*. But anybody would say shit if they were as clumsy as he was. Richard's hands were slick like butter because he always dropped things or almost fell due to his two left feet. But it was so cute to see him throw a tantrum.

"Shit, shit, shit!" he yelled.

"What happened?" I asked, hurrying outside to see what was the matter.

"I dropped the glass bowl," he said, looking at the shattered glass on the concrete. It was the bowl I had asked for to be placed in the middle of my kitchen table.

"No big deal," I said, giving him a kiss.

He was so patient and gentle. I felt protected and assured, but I believed Richard would leave me if he knew the truth about my past.

"Girl, that ain't none of his damn business," Maple would say when we had our girl chats. "That's your past," Maple fussed.

Maple loved Richard for me and she thought he was my husband.

I laughed it off.

Maple might have been right, but I felt he needed to know I was not always this poised and sweet. He came in and folded me up, making me gushy and weak.

We were playing cards one night, and I decided it would be the night I confessed my sins to him. As we played the card game, he had no idea that I had another game in mind—the game of losing or winning the love of my life. I had to allow the chips to fall where they may. I won the card game but showed no excitement after playing several Twenty-One games to avoid the difficult conversation.

"What's wrong?" Richard asked, taking my hand.

"Richard, I must tell you something," I said.

Richard squeezed my hand a little harder.

Damn, I thought. He was even assuring in the unknowing. I slowly took my hand from underneath his. I wished I had taken Maple's advice, but it was too late. I had his full attention as his concerned eyes grew on me.

"I...I was not always this good woman you see before you," I said. "I had a past."

"We all have a past," he said.

"But my past is....almost unbearable. I'm sorry that you might have been fooled, and if you knew the truth, you would never have looked my way."

"Clara, you can tell me."

"At one point, I was, I was a...woman who kind of lost her way and–

"You went by the name Honey," Richard said.

I leaned back in my chair and was speechless.

"I knew exactly who you were when I saw you at church. Clara, I have not been in the church all my life. I saw you plenty of times and prayed for you on the streets. I knew that if God could change me, he could change you or anybody. I used to hang out with the guys and sold some dope. I did dirt. I did a lot of shit. So, who am I to judge you?"

"So, you knew this entire time?" I asked.

"Yes, and I knew that you were my heartbeat too. Clara, you are *my Honey* now, and you have nothing to be ashamed of."

"You still want me?" I asked, shockingly.

"No. I *need* you," Richard said.

He took his hand and wiped the tear off my face, then we kissed the night away.

After the conversation, our love life sparked, but we remained abstinent. Richard was the man I knew I would cherish for the rest of my life. However, I was unsure about marriage, and the more we were around each other, the more I knew he would propose to me. He always dropped little hints and told me about our future together.

I had no desire to ever be married. I had one more serious conversation and was skeptical about how Richard would react. I sat him down. I didn't hesitate.

"Richard, I don't ever want to be married," I said.

"What?" he asked. He was lost for words. It was the last thing he expected to hear. "Huh? I'm not understanding," he said. "Is there another guy-

"Absolutely not," I said quickly. "Marriage isn't for me."

This is it, I thought. Richard was sure to leave me and find another woman to elope with so that he could fulfill his desires as he should. Even though it would have pained me for him to leave, I stood flat-footed on what I believed. I believed that marriage was not for me, and we did not need a piece of paper to define our love.

Richard was stunned, and the only thing he could say was shit. He stood up, looked around the room, and finally said, "Help me to understand. Have I not proven myself to be a great man?" he asked, raising his subtle voice. "I even paid for your plane ticket so you could be with your sister when she had her baby," he said.

Richard started naming all of the things that he did for me. I stopped him.

"You did a lot, and I appreciate you for everything. But Richard, marriage makes things more complicated," I said, expressing my fear of genuine commitment. "If you ever get tired of me, you can just leave."

"I would never get tired of you," Richard said. "I dream of you."

"And I dream of you too, but what if we get married and those sweet dreams turn into nightmares? Marriage changes things, and I am afraid I may be unable to give you what you want."

Richard got seriously quiet. He pondered before he began to speak. Then, he spoke with sincerity mixed with being pissed off.

"I saw my daddy give me so many siblings away from my mama. It was embarrassing before God. Half brothers there. Half sisters here. A nigga on the corner said I was his brother, and I never saw the nigga a day in my life until then. It is a disgrace! He was talking about how he knew my mama, our daddy's first and only wife, before he stepped out on her and became a rolling stone with a bunch of weak-minded women with hot coochies and a shitty can of beans. But my mama gave everything she had to him. I saw how she catered to him, but it wasn't good enough. I told myself I would never do a woman like my daddy did my mama. *Never!* I said I would get married, and my wife would carry *all* my kids. Don't you know how many women wanted to marry me, but I pushed them to the side and fell in love with a former whore!"

"Richard!!"

"Shit! I'm sorry. I'm so sorry. I didn't mean to say that. Clara, I got carried away. I'll just go. I will leave," Richard said. He was about to turn the doorknob and go. He stopped and said, "Wait a minute. You don't want to get married because I can just leave when things get heated."

"Exactly," I said. "Richard, I'm not upset at you. You have every right to be angry and pissed off-

He shut me up and kissed me.

"I'm not going to allow the lack of marriage to stop me from loving you. I just can't imagine you carrying another man's child."

"I get it, but-

"Do you still want to be the mother of my children?" he asked.

"Yes."

"Then that is good enough for me."

"Richard realized I might have been right about marriage. After we had our two boys, Joey and Phillip, he went on and married twice and got divorced twice," Ms. Honey said. "Still, to this day, he says his marriages didn't work because I am his true wife." Honey laughed.

When Honey finished telling her story, she called Maple.

"Maple, I hate that you don't feel good. Is there anything else I can do for you?" Honey said, speaking on the phone.

"No, I'm good. Tell Richard I will see him another time. I wonder if he plans to propose to you after all these years," Maple said, laughing before she started coughing.

"Uh, huh, that's what happens when you are messy," Honey said. "Take care, and I will check on you later."

"Anything you want me to help you with?" Ivy asked.

"No, I'm good."

Honey was setting the dinner table. Richard has been out of town helping his brothers do some work around their dad's old house, turning it into a transitional home for displaced youth.

"I'm glad I'll be meeting Richard this evening," Ivy said. "I can tell in your eyes that you love that man."

I don't know why you didn't marry him, Ivy thought.

There was a knock on the door, and Richard arrived on time as he said he was.

Honey opened the door.

"My wife!" Richard said, grabbing Honey around her thick hips and kissing her. "Ooooh, I miss you so much."

"I miss you too, Mama," Joey said, surprising Honey.

"Joey!" Honey nearly pushed Richard out of the way to reach her oldest son.

"Hey, I decided to catch a ride with Dad and come and see you, too."

"I should have known something was up. Take off your coat and wash up. I got dinner ready."

"Smelling good. Looking good," Richard said, rubbing his hands. He traveled miles away, and all he wanted was Honey and Honey's home-cooked meal. "And who are you?" he asked Ivy.

"This is Ivy," Honey said, smiling.

Joey stuck his head out the bathroom door and admired what he saw.

"Damn," Joey whispered. He cleaned his hands, fixed his shirt, and introduced himself. "And I am Joey," he said, "Mama, you didn't tell me you had such a gorgeous friend."

"Thanks," Ivy said. *And she did not tell me she had such a handsome son,* Ivy thought.

After dinner, Ivy sat outside to get some fresh air. She enjoyed laughing at the two old love birds, Ms. Honey and Richard. But she could not keep her eyes off Joey at the dinner table, and Joey tried not to do the same. Occasionally, they would catch each other eyeing one another and act like they were listening to Richard's jokes or long stories.

"Hey, I didn't know you were out here," Joey said. He left some clothes in the car and went to get them. He was startled at the awkward encounter. "Sorry for my dad's corny jokes," he said, "imagine a fourteen-hour drive with him."

"It's fine. I think you have wonderful parents," Ivy said. "You are truly blessed to have them."

"I am. I am a pretty lucky guy. So—are you single by chance?"

"I am. I am very single," Ivy laughed.

"How about I take you on a date to get to know each other better?

Ivy looked to her left at Brian's house, smiled gracefully, and said, "Sure."

"Maple, are you okay?" Honey asked on the phone.

"Yes, I'm just watching Ivy and Joey on your front porch," Maple said, peeking through the curtains. "It looks like they're having a good time talking. Ivy might be your daughter-in-law."

"Girl, bye."

THIRTY-TWO

Joey pulled out Ivy's chair so that she could be seated at a steakhouse restaurant in the downtown area. Joey was a pleasant surprise, so Ivy accepted his invitation to dinner.

"Thank you," Ivy said, taking her seat. She was shy yet excited that she could go on a date with someone so genuine as Joey.

"You look absolutely stunning," Joey said. It was one of many compliments of the day.

Ivy smiled and read the menu.

"Order whatever you would like," Joey said.

Ivy was undoubtedly done with Brian, and for the past few days, she forgot he existed.

"Do you prefer white or red wine?" Joey asked.

"Red, for sure."

They ordered their food and then started getting to know each other better.

"Well, as you know, I work in real estate development and was just offered a job in tech," Joey said as he smoothed out his black jacket.

"Well, I am just an assistant manager at a boutique," Ivy said, then giggled.

"Don't downgrade your accomplishments," Joey said. "That is a big deal. Mind you, you weren't working there long."

Joey was smart and savvy with a business sense of how to run things. He knew how to open doors and create his own way. Joey was an ambitious man who was focused. His characteristics were compelling, gentle, and firm. She also knew he was raised by a strong woman and had a close relationship with his dad.

"That is true," Ivy said. "So, why are you single?" Ivy asked, taking a sip of her wine. She had to get the burning question off her lips. She knew there had to be something wrong. Joey was neat, worked out, kept a nice bald fade, had glowing skin, and was a pretty boy who could fix a car and work in the corporate world.

Joey took a huff and sipped his wine before he answered her question.

"I am quite a generous guy. I do not want to toot my own horn, but I give and offer a lot, and what I find in most women is that they don't value or cherish what I do for them. They just —excuse me, they give me sex and think I am supposed to be satisfied as they enjoy the fruits of my labor and spend my money. I thought nothing of it when I was younger, but as I matured, I wanted a wife, a woman I could build with. A woman that if I lost everything, I would be confident and assured that she would help me build it right back up. Truth is, that happened to me. My bank account was in the negative before, and my credit was shot to shit because I was too nice and far too giving. This will sound absurd, but in my last relationship, I purchased her a brand new car, a Lexus," he said.

Ivy was about to damn near choke on her bread.

"And she still cheated," Joey said as the waiter placed their food on the table. He whispered, "Thank you." Then, he kept talking. "To my fault. I have always been gullible to think that every one of my past girlfriends was—a friend, that no matter what happened, we would still be cool. Much like my parents are," he said, laughing. "And I think we can agree that their relationship is one of a kind."

Once Ivy got over the news that he purchased a brand new car for his girlfriend and said it was no big deal, she said, "Well, you definitely deserve someone who would love you for you."

Joey cut into his steak. "So, are you saying that you are not trying to be that person?" He said. "How's your food?" he asked, afraid he might have been too straightforward. Joey was not playing around. He was thirty-two and looking for marriage.

Ivy felt like this was too good to be true. A couple of months ago, she was a messy mistress who was kicked out of a married man's house and cried on the front lawn, picking up her things from the grass. In her mind, there was no way that God would send her an angel with good credit her way so soon.

"I do, however. I am not looking to rush into anything," Ivy said honestly.

"I completely understand," Joey said, smiling.

The night was going smoothly, and the connection was unforced. Joey looked like his dad, but he had Honey's ways, and she thought it was nearly perfect.

"So, would you like to go to the Spring Ball with me?" Joey asked.

"Isn't that like two weeks away?" Ivy asked.

The Spring Ball was the talk of the town, and everybody seemed to be going. Before she answered, someone texted her phone.

"Interesting," she whispered, then refocused her attention back to Joey, who pulled out his credit card to pay for the dinner. "I would love to go," Ivy said. "It should be fun."

When Ivy got to Honey's house, she wasted no time before she called Maple.

"How was your date?" Maple asked.

"So, Honey told you," Ivy said.

"Of course she did."

"It was great, but I'm calling you for a favor."

"What is it?"

"I need you to make one more dress for the Spring Ball. Joey invited me to go."

Maple went silent.

"Ms. Maple?"

"Ivy, the ball is two weeks away and I don't have time. Don't you get a discount at the boutique? I am tired. I love what I do, but I am tired."

"Ms. Maple, please. You are the only one I know that can make me look beyond gorgeous. Please, Ms. Maple. *Please*."

Maple waited to answer. "Okay. I can see what I can do."

"Thank you, you are the best!"

"Uh, huh. Come by tomorrow after work with your happy ass."

THIRTY-THREE

The Spring Ball had arrived, and everyone was at Honey's house taking pictures.

"Tally, you look so stunning," Ivy said. Ivy wore her long navy, sparkle gown.

"Thanks! Even though I am going alone this year. It will not stop my shine," Tally said. "Now, take my picture over here."

"Sure, no problem," Joey said sarcastically. He was tired of taking pictures of Tally, who criticized every photo and made him retake it a few times because her head was slanted the wrong way, her eyes were not that open, or her shoes were cropped out.

"Okay, okay, let me get a picture of the couple by the stairs," Honey said proudly. She was elated to see her son and Ivy going out together. "One, two, and three," Honey said, and she snapped the picture on her iPhone. "This will be printed and placed on my wall."

"Really, Mama," Joey said.

Tally peeked outside and saw Maple making her way across the street. "Okay, Maple is coming," she said.

Maple knocked on the door, and Honey welcomed her inside her living room. Honey said, "They look so good."

Maple acted like she woke up on the wrong side of the bed. She did not speak before saying, "Ivy, that is not the dress *I* made for you. Where is the dress that I made for you?" She asked, holding her hand on her hip. "Because I know damn well I didn't slave at the last minute and you ain't put on the dress that *I* made you. Do you hear me? Where is the damn dress that *I* made?"

"Hey, Mama," Jasmine said, coming into the room in the flowing golden dress her mama made.

Maple was shocked as her bottom jaw dropped open, and tears began to flow.

Maple said, "Jasmine, you're wearing the dress *I* made."

"Yes, Mama," Jasmine said softly. Then, she went and hugged her, whispering, "I love you, Mama, and I'm so sorry."

"I'm so sorry, too," Maple cried.

Ivy and Tally tried hard not to ruin their make-up as they witnessed a tearful reunion. Honey shed happy tears with them as she saw God work before her very eyes.

"You look so beautiful," Maple said. "*Oh, my baby.*"

Ivy and Joey had a great time at The Spring Ball. Ivy saw why it was the talk of the town. If given the chance, she would go back, but the time seemed too short. Joey pulled up in the driveway and parked. He got out and opened the door for Ivy, then guided her up the stairs on the porch.

"I really enjoyed myself with you tonight," Ivy said. "Thanks for inviting me."

"I'm glad you went with me," Joey said, adjusting his black tux.

They leaned in to kiss, but a loud thud next door interrupted their romance. Brian slumped on his porch and held his chest.

"Help, help," Brian screamed out. "Aw—

Ivy and Joey ran over to Brian's yard to check on him. Brian had his hand on his chest with a towel pressed against him. He was bloody and was on the verge of passing out.

"Oh, my God! What happened?" Ivy asked

"Looks like he was stabbed," Joey said, whipping out his phone to call an ambulance.

Without hesitation, Ivy took off her shawl and tried to help control his bleeding. She was terrified for Brian as she tried to get him to calm down.

"You're going to be okay. Brian, listen—I need you to stay awake."

"Help is on the way," Joey said.

"Brian...Brian-

Ivy was in the hospital waiting room as she anticipated hearing the news on Brian's condition. She knew that her relationship with him was rough. Still, she did stop wishing for anything terrible to happen to him. She would have never guessed that after a magical night, she would be in her navy blue gown, all dolled up in a hospital, to be there for a man she hated who treated her less than a stray dog.

"Are you his wife," the nurse asked.

"No, I am his—friend," Ivy said, "I was the one who helped him until the ambulance arrived," she explained.

"Oh, okay, well—he is in stable condition. He sustained some injuries to his chest, but he will live."

"Good."

"You may go see him. He's in room 219," she said, pointing her pin toward where she should go.

Ivy tipped towards the room and was skeptical about Brian's reaction. She wasn't even sure if he knew what had happened to him, for he almost passed out a few times.

She saw him lying on the bed, resting. Brian felt her presence and opened his eyes. He showed a slight grin on his face, lucky to be alive. Had the knife gone deeper, it would have purged into his heart.

"I guess it pays to be heartless," Brian whispered. He still joked, slightly embarrassed of how he handled Ivy. "I deserved this."

"No, you did not," Ivy said. She sat next to him on the right side of the bed. "What happened?" she asked, looking at his bandaged chest.

"My wife came to town, and we heatedly argued. She tried to kill me," Brian said.

"I am so sorry about that," Ivy said sincerely.

Brian turned his head and saw that Ivy showed compassion. He said, "Ivy, I am so sorry for what I did to you. Would you forgive me?"

Ivy said, "Of course. We were both in the wrong, you know?"

There was a slight silence as she watched Brian trying to get comfortable on the bed.

"Would you mind adjusting my pillow?" Brian asked as he pulled himself up a little.

Ivy helped so that his head could rest in a better position.

"Thank you," Brian said, "you didn't have to save my life."

"You're welcome, and Brian, take it easy, okay?" Ivy said. She found the perfect time to leave him and go home to get some rest herself. It was nearly 3 A.M., and her feet were sore.

"Ivy, I hope you find a man that will treat you as you are supposed to be treated," he said. "I hope life treats you kindly."

"Thanks. And I wish you the very best from here on out," Ivy said.

THIRTY-FOUR

Honey sat in her dressing room. This was the moment that she anticipated most of her life. *Where Hearts Are Found* by Clara "Honey" Brown was published and released in the bookstores. After marketing, the book flew off the shelves and made her *New York's Best Time Seller.*

In the next hour or so, she will be interviewed in front of an audience that includes everyone she loves.

Honey finished signing her last book when she heard a soft knock on the door.

"Come in," Honey said, thinking it would be the make-up artist.

"Hey, sister!" Erica said. "You know I was not going to miss your big moment."

"Erica!"

They hugged and chatted like little girls at Mama's house, even though her sister was Dr. Erica S. Brown. Honey almost forgot where she was as they laughed loudly and danced excitedly around the dressing room. They were mere images of their mom and aunts.

"I think we should quiet down now," Erica said.

"Did you read my book?" Honey asked, sitting down.

"Of course I did. I knew you could do anything that you put your mind to. I never doubted you," Erica said. "I just thank God my old eyes can still see." She laughed. "Here, I have something for you." Erica went into her purse and pulled out a small wrapped box.

"What is this," Honey asked, taking the gift.

"Hurry up and open it," Erica said, "acting like Mama."

Honey giggled and opened the gift, and she was astonished beyond her imagination, just as she believed that her life could not get any better.

Honey finally said, "This is the pearl necklace. Erica, I thought the necklace was gone."

"I kept it," Erica said. "I knew if Aunt Gayle had a hold of it, it would have been gone. I had it the entire time, thinking I would surprise you when I got married first, but marriage wasn't in my future," Erica giggled. "Don't cry, Honey. I want you to have it now."

"It's like I can feel our ancestors. They will be with me on that stage tonight. Aunt Sweetie, Aunt Gayle, and...*Mama*.

"Yes, they will be."

Honey sat in the green chair on the stage with her long, flowing purple gown that Maple had created, looking out into the audience. She was poised yet nervous when the Black woman interviewer asked her questions about her book.

"I love you, God Mommy!" Marcus screamed, forcing her to relax.

"I love you too," Honey called back. The rest of the interview went perfectly as if she had been in the spotlight for years.

She acknowledged everyone and told them how each person played a special part in her life: her late family, Erica, Maple, Richard, her sons, Marcus, Tally, and Jasmine. Honey thanked Ivy for helping her make a dream come true. She said that Ivy was a unique Angel sent to help.

Joey hugged Ivy around her shoulder, kissed her on the cheek quickly, and grinned proudly at his mama.

"What do you want people to know that you believe is so important?" the interviewer asked.

Honey lifted the mic to her lips and said, "I want people to know that it is never too late to live your dreams. Do not allow circumstances to hinder you. I am a school dropout who became an author. It's not too late to be anything you want to be," she said as she rubbed her pearl necklace. Then she looked at Richard and said, "It's not even too late to get married."

Richard nearly fainted. He was finally going to marry the woman of his dreams.

"Nicely put," the interviewer said. "Last question. Will you be writing any more books?"

"Yes. My next book will be co-written with my best friend, Anna Washington, known as Maple. We will write an autobiography about our lives in hopes of inspiring others to never give up."

Jasmine hugged Maple.

"Do you know the name of the book?"

"Yes. The book will be titled, *"The Life of Maple and Honey."*

MAPLE AND HONEY

About the Author

Gerald D. Johnson, born in Mobile, Alabama, writes fiction based on Afican-American characters. Johnson writes bold narratives to inspire and entertain. Johnson writes in all genres and dares to be different and courageous, introducing stories to stir up vast emotions. Johnson is the writer of the books, The Eye to My Storms, Alabama Sunrise, and A Dream Deferred.

Instagram: brothagerald